Celestial Blue Skies

Celestial Blue Skies

Maggie Collins

Battered Suitcase Press

Celestial Blue Skies

Battered Suitcase Press
http://www.batteredsuitcasepress.com

An imprint of Vagabondage Press LLC
PO Box 3563
Apollo Beach, Florida 33572
http://www.vagabondagepress.com

First edition printed in the United States of America and the United Kingdom, April 2014

10 9 8 7 6 5 4 3 2 1

Front cover art by Sritangphoto/ Voronin76/ Nikita Vasilchenko.. Cover designed by Maggie Ward.

Celestial Blue Skies

Celestial Blue Skies is dedicated
to Uncle Romiere Auzenne.

Chapter 1

Come and Fetch Your Mama

Celeste

"No God-fearing, decent woman wants to have a bad reputation in a small, one-traffic-light town like Belle Place, Louisiana," my grandmother, Maymay, always tells me. I think about that light and my mother, Tut, the whore of Belle Place. I can't stop that light from directing traffic in such a lonely town, and I can't stop my mom from ho-ing in the streets in this town, either. All I can do is pedal next to my Maymay.

When I look at Maymay, I feel her energy, and I think about the things that add life to the quiet sky: like my Uncle T-Red with his washboard scratching to the beat, my grandfather, T-Man, pumping the accordion while T-Red's wife, Bumblebee, fills the kitchen with the smells of hot boudin, crackling, hog head cheese, and all kinds of cakes. My sisters and cousins sing and dance to songs about stolen chickens, stolen women, crazy women like my mama, and crazy French words I don't want to know.

"Come and fetch your daughter." I give Maymay the message, plain and simple, along with the mail. My grandmother slicks her black hair into her everyday ponytail and puts on a clean, pink housedress with white tennis shoes, now covered with dirt from the dusty road.

I know that I don't have to answer her when she talks to herself. All I need to do is ride my bike ahead and watch out for cars. Every time one passes, I yell, "Car!" We go down to the gravel edge of the ditch and wait for the car to speed past us.

We look down the highway that looks like it never ends. She wipes the dripping sweat from her face with the clean dishrag she carries in the huge pocket shaped like a yellow daisy.

"I want a cold Pepsi," Maymay shouts.

I ride my bike. It feels like I'm flying away from Belle Place, my mama, and her reputation. I'm flying past the red light to get to my own place. My eyes are closed, and my bare feet lift between each strong pedal.

We pass the houses near the store. There are rows and rows of "sharp shoot" houses. Some people call them shotgun houses. Maymay calls them sharp shoot houses, because a sharp shooter can shoot from the front door to the back door without hitting one piece of wood—only air.

They line the street one by one like green, plastic GI Joe soldiers ready for an imaginary battle. They all look alike, but they are different colors. Some are yellow, brown, and even purple. Their colors are the only thing that makes them look different. Each has a front door, a few windows, and a back door. Someone is behind a screened porch reading *The Daily Belle Place News*.

"*Comment ca vas*," a man's voice says.

"*Ca vas bien*," Maymay says. "They always want to talk," she adds as she picks up speed, trying to end the quickly moving conversation. "There ain't nothing to talk about in this dead-ass town. The newspaper that he steady reading ain't got nothing but a few boring stories. The only important news is the dead folk. That's the only news you need to know, so you can pay your respect. I wish I could drive. I would grab Tut and drive her clean out of this place and park her where nobody knows her. I would let her start over, but you can't drive away from a bad name," Maymay says.

Mama can't drive away from sleeping with married men, showing her tits to young boys, or having sex with drunks for Moon Pies and Honey Buns behind Smitty's Shack corner store. Mama can't change who she is. Mama can't change who we are.

"We have to cross the road now to get to the other side. Get behind me! These cars pass fast. They don't care about us. They will run us over like an old mama dog." A green Monte Carlo zooms by, almost knocking Maymay off her tired feet. She looks both ways, and we cross the road.

Soon, we can hear Mama shouting. My mama Tut's long legs are the first thing I see since she's got shorts all the way up to her thighs. Her sandy hair is pulled back in a long, thick ponytail that she is holding and running her fingers through. She yells, "Yeah y'all, that's right. Nare-o-one of us leaving until me and Papoo get our money back." Every time she screams, her body leans like a cold drink bottle that has been hit by one of those white gravel rocks that are beneath our feet.

Papoo, my mama's so called best friend as Maymay calls her, is playing cards with four other people who are waiting for their clothes in the washeteria. The group of card players continues to play pinochle and watch out for the cops that Mrs. Smitty has threatened to call. As soon as the police arrive, I know Papoo and all the card players, like Willie and Monkey Man, will take their money and run, forgetting about my mama and the show she has created for herself and all of them.

My mama says, "I'm tired of coming here with all of these jacked-up prices for stuff that ain't even worth it."

Mama is playing with the end of her ponytail, which stops just above her waist. She then fights off ants that are on her ashy shins to suck sugar from a strawberry soda that she spilled on her legs.

Mama looks at Mrs. Smitty, who eyes her from the window of the store. Mama screams at her, "Look at her over there! I see you peeping, you old, dried-up bitch. You charge more than town and don't want to give people they money back when they find bugs in y'all stuff, like the baby roaches me and Papoo found in our Moon Pies. I'm sick of y'all cheating poor, honest folks of Belle Place."

Smitty's daughter, Joyce, keeps a watchful eye on my mama from her mother's carport. Mama is not allowed to go in the store when Mrs. Smitty is there. She can only use the machines outside.

"I'm the only one who can say something about it on account I own my own land with my people. I don't live in one of them rackety houses out back. I'm tired of ya'll cheating people who can't fight back. It would be one thing if y'all was white, but y'all black, like us," my mama says.

Mrs. Robinson pulls her clothes out of the dryer. "You right, baby. I pay $3 for stuff I can pay $2 for in town. That little dollar goes further in town. They greedy for money in that store, and Mrs. Smitty be watching everybody like a hawk. I'm not going to spend another dollar in there," she says and folds her clothes on the clean white table.

My mother repeats everything that the customers and Papoo talk about when the owners are not around. Only my mother's voice is so loud that I have to cover my ears. "Mr. Smitty is fresh. He always be trying to feel on my breasts." Mama lifts braless breasts with her bony fingers. Her hard nipples show through her shirt. She raises her voice. "He be eyeing me all the time."

Giving her legs a deep scratch that leaves white marks, she looks at Mrs. Smitty, who stares from the store window. "Did he tell you about that, you old biddy? Did he tell you? That's why you don't want me in there. You hate to face the truth about that little weasel you call a husband. You know it's not me. You know it's him. You know it. It's not my fault I look good. A pretty girl ain't safe in this town with perverts like your husband, baby."

My mama stands there in her blue jean cutoffs, plastic purple flip flops, and purple tank top. "I don't need to go in your old store, anyway. They ain't nothing worth buying in that crusty old store. All that stuff stale, anyway. Me and Papoo have to throw away a lot of stuff Mr. Smitty gives us because it's stale. You hear that? Stale. Instead of looking at me, you need to be looking at your expiration dates and throwing that stale shit you call food away." Mama rolls her eyes and begins to laugh at her own joke.

Maymay slaps my mama so hard that her cheap, pink, plastic, lightning-shaped earrings fly through the air. "Stop trying to show off, you little heifer. Carry ya narrow yeller tail back to the house. You don't even own them hand-me-down shorts on your hot little ass," Maymay says. The crowd bursts into laughter.

"If I could, I would take the life I gave you from you, because you don't know how to live it decent. Papoo, you ought to be sorry for making this girl cut up. You know she simple. You smarter than her. You just bad. You know I ain't got no way to come back here and fetch this crazy girl. We got all them children back there to take care of, and you making her act up. T-Man's at work with T-Red. Nobody's back home to help me in the day. You know that," Maymay says. She looks at Papoo and all of the card players eye-to-eye, wanting them to feel bad for what they did to my mama.

For the first time, Papoo stops and turns and looks up to where Maymay is standing. "I'm sorry, ma'am. It won't happen again. I tried to stop her. *Mais,* you know how Tut is once she starts cutting up. You can't stop her. As pretty as Tut is, I never have to worry about her with my old man, Bo. He says Belle Place can have all Tut tuney. He says if you cut her down the middle, some crazy kind of black juice would pop out of her. He swears he done saw her spit it out before. She just ain't normal." Papoo says as she and the card players laugh once more at Bo's joke.

Papoo smiles, revealing her new gold tooth covered with a cursive letter "P." She laughs so hard that she tips the cigar box filled with pennies, nickels, quarters, and dimes. They continue to play their illegal game in the deep shadows of the washeteria, not caring about the money, only the laughter and fun my mother brings to their game of pinochle.

Maymay pulls Mama by her long ponytail and then shouts at me. "Celeste, go get what I need so I can go back to ma house and fix ma lunch." I empty my mama's basket, which is filled with warm clothes and stolen merchandise. My mama stole the items from the outside snack machines that Papoo and her know how to rob.

"Pay that lady for everything this girl done stole," she tells me. She hands me a $10 roll of quarters from her black leather purse. I run as quickly as I can through the white gravel driveway with the basket of stolen merchandise and the money to pay for it.

Mrs. Smitty says that I am "old," which means I am young, but I act like an old lady. I smile and say hello and do as Maymay told me to do. Whenever I can, I clean Ms. Smitty's property around her store by picking up bottles that I collect as well as other trash. In exchange for my hard work, she gives me penny candy. I try to make up for what my mama does.

We are now making our way back home. I don't look at Mama, not even once, because I don't want to get in trouble with Maymay by starting her up again. It's strange, but my mama gets calm next to my Maymay. She is looking at my hair and smiling, but I am riding my bike and ignoring her like I would a stray, playful dog. I pretend that she isn't there, and I stay focused. It's best for all of us.

The crowd evaporates like a puddle of water on hot cement. I hear someone shout, "I think that she is 100 percent right. We need more people like that to stand up for the little people back ya. Nobody ever tells them like it is. Nobody! Just Tut! She ain't all that crazy like people make her out to be."

Mama is like a red sock. Belle Place is like white laundry. Nobody places a red, bleeding sock in their clean, white laundry. She doesn't take well to the roosters crowing like we do. She doesn't like the wash pan and the fiddles and the slow French songs of the day, like we do. She bleeds the laundry with her made-up songs, art, and fussing. I dare not smile back at her as she admires the crooked plaits and mismatched barrettes that she placed in my hair this morning. She wants to change me and Maymay's world of straight greased plaits, mail, French, work, cooking, and Saturday zydeco on the front porch.

She wants crooked, tangled ponytails, made-up songs, arguments, belly dancing, and gypsy music. All those things don't belong. I, as a twelve-year-old living in 1985, know that.

Mama is behind us. She is looking at the pink buttercups that Maymay says stink up the house when my mama places them in Pepsi bottles and lines them along the windowsill. Her bouquet grows each time we move near the ditch to avoid quickly passing cars.

Maymay sings to a strange, cool breeze in the middle of July. The song is so familiar. She sings it to babies in the rocking chair. The rocking chair and song are glued to my brain…

Bells on my fingers
Rings on my toes
I shall have music wherever I go

I lift my bare feet one more time, and I dream about crossing that red light hanging in my blue sky.

Chapter 2

Maymay and T-Man Bastille

Maymay

We don't have many visitors out here in the country. The milkman comes on Mondays. Mr. Fred, the fruit man, comes on Saturdays to sell his fruit from a maroon 1980 pickup truck with a two-tone brown and white camper on the back. He's got oranges, apples, and grapes. I always buy the cheapest things: oranges and apples. Every child in ma house gets an orange.

Teefee drives by from the Mount Mariah Baptist Church to sell her pecan candy, sweet dough pie, and barbecue dinners whenever her church is trying to raise money, which is all the time.

I like to buy pecan candies. *Mais,* they're not good all the time. Sometimes they stick to ma mouth. We don't make a fuss about it 'cause they too high to throw away. I make them children eat 'em, sticky or not. You got to know how to save money when you got so many mouths to feed.

Ma husband treat people for they sickness. I don't like all them people on ma property. I never let nobody in ma house, but I let him meet them by the road, and he treats them. Ma husband can tell when somebody coming to get healed. He always says, "I can feel somebody coming today. I can feel it, Maymay,"

That man there loves to talk about the old times. He says, "People used to come by me to get treated a lot back in the days when people worried about their neighbors and came to see about you. We would have big parties and kill hogs and visit with everybody. Now, people don't believe that God can heal them through *traiteurs*. Now, they go straight to the doctor. But, I get the feeling when people who got belief coming. I get the feeling," he says. T-Man looks out the window. He can't see nobody coming, but he the feeling that somebody is coming. He looks out of his bedroom window at the long, empty road out yonder.

Soon, the children yell, "Company!"

I am cleaning snap beans under ma favorite spot, ma tree. "That look like Mr. Plaisance," I say.

"I caught you some brim, Maymay. Look how nice." Mr. Plaisance lifts the ice chest and shows me the big brim he caught.

"Oh yeah, they're nice. I'm going to make a fish *coubion* tonight with corn and snap beans," I say.

"Oh, that sounds like some good eating," he says.

Mr. Plaisance puts the fish in the dishpan one of the children brings for me.

He used to be our landlord. T-Man worked with him as a field hand in the sugar cane fields. He bought our place for us. It took me and T-Man fifteen years to pay it back, but we paid him back every last red cent.

Mr. Plaisance says, "I caught *beaucoup* fish today. I know how much you like brim, so I made sure that I passed here to bring you some, Maymay. You can't buy that in the store, you know."

"Thank you. I got some tomatoes from ma garden. Maymay can pick you some," T-Man says.

Mr. Plaisance says, "I don't want anything, just my good name. Thank you. I have a little toothache, T-Man. Do you think you can pray for my toothache?" Mr. Plaisance stands next to his Ford pickup truck, holding his jaw with a clean white handkerchief. He has a huge cowboy hat on. He looks at the rosary that he holds in his hand. He just like me; he carry the rosary everywhere he go.

T-Man tells him, "I will pray for you. You know what they say. It's all about believing. The belief does the trick, every time." He touches the side of Mr. Plaisance's face and prays to himself. He takes the sickness from Mr. Plaisance's face and shakes it to the ground. Like all *traiteurs*, T-Man don't take nothing for his prayers.

Soon the prayer is over. Mr. Plaisance looks at T-Man eye-to-eye and says, "T-Man, you know the last time you prayed for me my back was hurting. I went to the doctor, and it didn't help. Your prayer helped. I held this same rosary in my hand." He looks at his callused hand holding that there rosary. "Why don't people come by you like they used to?" he asks ma husband.

"Things changed over the years. Treating's not the same, now. People don't have the belief. The belief does the trick, every time. It's the belief. I mostly just treat ma family. I get *moogreay, la tea zon*, sassafras, and other teas to help us get over our colds and other sickness. That's why people call me T-Man."

Mr. Plaisance is one of the few people in Belle Place that don't see ma husband as Frenchy and backwards. A lot of people in this town don't like us 'cause we stay to our self. We don't like meddling in other people business. I don't let no women in ma house. Ma mama always told me never let a bitch in your house. They know how to carry hoodoo with 'em, and they cause too much confusion.

I don't like to fool with the white people too much because I don't want nobody thinking I'm trying to pass. I just want me and ma family to ma self.

Mr. Plaisance now takes that huge hat from his head and kisses the Blessed Virgin Mary that he wears around his neck.

T-Man shakes his hand and says, "I hope you make out all right with that tooth."

"I'll let you know how I made out," Mr. Plaisance says. He slams the truck door and speeds down the road. All that is left is the dust and gravel.

I am in the business of cleaning the fish. Tut is swinging strong and hard on the homemade swing under the huge oak tree. Even though that gal is 26 and has four kids, she loves to swing and always has.

"I'm going all the way to the sky," she sings as she stretches her long, skinny legs higher than the lowest limb of the tree.

Me and ma husband reared four children together, including Tut, T-Red, Billy (who died in Vietnam), and Joseph, who left to go in the army in California and never came back. *Mais,* we never heard from him again. It is a big mystery. T-Man and me talk about it some nights in our little bedroom together. We think that a small, country boy like Joseph probably ran into a crowd of thieves or mean people. When we gather on our knees every night in the living room as a family, we pray for him to come back. It's been eight years since he left.

Tut is swinging under the tree, singing with her take-around tape player. She is singing Diana Ross. It's a song about a fella turning a gal upside down. Celeste tells me the song is called "Upside Down." She's singing her little ass off in that tree. She looks like skin, bones, and wild hair.

She thinks the world of Diana Ross because she has long, thick hair like that girl. That's what T-Red told me the other day. He showed me the red Big Chief tablet she keeps that woman's songs in. Bumblebee sits with me and Celeste as she cleans the green beans that I was working on.

Bumblebee says, "Tut got four children, but she still a child. Only one of her children been baptized—that's Celeste, the only one with sense. Hattie is four and never been baptized. Mattie four, never been baptized. Tiny is ten, never been baptized. And Celeste was baptized twelve years ago by Father Etienne, but he told Tut he wouldn't baptize another illegitimate child again, less she could bring the men forward who made the babies. I say that curse on Tut and her children could be broke, if you let them get baptized at my church," Bumblebee says.

She grabs more green beans from the white bucket next to me. I say, "He wanted to stop Tut from having sex with all them men in Belle Place. Her ways would have consequences, is what he told me. If he lets Tut get away with it, we will have a town filled with fatherless children with no religion. It would be the end of Belle Place. Our town will go to hell like the rest of the country. Father said Belle Place only one of the few places people still really believe in God. He doesn't want bad blood on his hands," I say. I smile at Celeste. She's cleaning the green beans faster than Bumblebee. She's such a hardworking child.

I say, "This family's always been Catholic. I'm still praying that Tut will find out who her children daddies is or them men will come out of the woodworks and show they faces to me. I pray the rosary every day."

Father Etienne really hurt me. Still, I am not going to leave ma church. I am going to be Catholic until the day I die. I say ma rosary every day. Sometimes, I say it more than three times a day.

I know about people who can give Tut a special tea so that she could've got her period and pass her babies, but I made sure that Tut had all of her babies like a woman.

Every time Tut would remind me about that tea, I would say, "I can't pray to the Blessed Mother Mary enough for a child you done left in limbo. I would have to stay on ma knees all day and night, and I would bore a hole in that strong cypress floor. I would wear that rocking chair all the way to the dirt ground under ma house. We enough women and children here; we'll help you with your li'l baby."

I tell Celeste and Bumblebee, "After all of these years of kindness, that's all Mr. Plaisance wants, his good name. He says it all the time like clockwork. But you, Tut, you want to ruin T-Man's good name. You're giving all them messy people something to talk about in this dead town. You done had four children. You think you would stop at one. If you don't know, we're poor."

Tut is a *petain*. That means whore in Creole. I try my best not to use bad language in front of those kids, but they probably know what it means by now.

Tut got that music blasted all the way to the sky. I throw fish guts into the white slop bucket. I want to throw it at her. I look at her, and she got nothing better to do but sing her ass off,

I've never seen anyone dance in a swing, but Tut dancing her little ass off in the swing. She dancing and having fun doing it.

When I am done cleaning the fish, I tell Celeste, "Go throw these guts over yonder in the trash barrel. I don't want no green flies by ma house. It's enough your nasty mama sinful, disgusting self in ma house."

I turn the tape player off with a heavy, dirty finger. I tell Tut, "If you weren't ma kin, I would get rid of you. Throw you in the trash barrel with these guts," I hold the last fish head in ma hand. I am ready to pitch it at her. "You're ma blood, so I'm going to help you with your simple-minded self. Just don't push me." Tut deliberately puts the song on again to try ma nerves. I take the tape player and slap Tut's hand with the fish head.

When Tut tries to take the tape player from ma slimy hands, I tell her, "Take it. I dare you. I'll knock the shit out of you. Better yet, I'll get T-Red to beat you."

Tut sits in the swing, knock-kneed. She looks at the tape player like she studying about it. She starts swinging again. Her long, bony legs are up yonder to the sky. She says, "High in the sky. I'm going high as the sky." She sings her "Upside Down" song again without the tape player.

I know you got that apple peel
You always play in my field
I'm crazy that you are mind
As long as my sun shine
There's a place in my field for you
And that's fine

"Well, Maymay, if she don't know nothing else, she know how to mess up a song. Tut says that's her song." Bumblebee laughs and hands me ma green beans.

"I don't feel like fighting with her today. She's gonna bring ma pressure up, something I don't need. I'm getting too old for Tut foolishness. She's never gon' grow up. We got to go watch *Hee Haw*, anyway, and fry these fish. You know I like ma show. We're gonna eat good, today. She can swing her ass off out here, for all I care. I bet she be eating cush cush for supper." With all ma fight gone, I put the tape player back by Tut. I take ma fish and ma beans.

Tut stops swinging and looks up at the sky and then at Celeste. Celeste knows what to do—ignore her.

While Celeste is cleaning the stinky fish, she is singing and shaking her long hair like some high yeller movie star.

Tut tells Celeste, "Watch how high I can go, Celeste. Watch. Watch. Just sit there and watch me." I nod ma head so Celeste can look. She doesn't want to look, then she steals a peak at her mama. Tut smells like cheap rose perfume and wears a pretty, short, pink dress. Her daughter is covered in fish scales and blood. I want Celeste to look at her.

"Look at her one last time, Celeste. She is what we are not. We are women folk with a dinner to cook and children to look after. I don't want you to end up like her," I say, and I mean it. "Mr. Plaisance don't have to tell me about his name." I wash ma hands with the garden hose. "If I hear anybody talking about him, I will give him a piece of ma mind. If it hadn't been for him, we would be in a rent house."

I say, "Mr. Smitty—that's not a good man. Tut gives her breast to him for taffy, soda water, and Moon Pies. She tells ya'll it's only a tiddy tap. That's a nasty old man. I don't want any of you grandchildren going there without me. Don't y'all mess with that old man. You gon' catch the worms."

I want Celeste to look at her *mon*. Soon she will be a woman just like her mama. I just hope and pray she don't end up like her, a used-up *petain*.

I tell Celeste, "Your granddaddy and Mr. Plaisance respect each other. They both got good names, no matter what people think. If you live a good life, your mama's bad name won't follow you. Worry about you. Now go take ma clothes off of the line, so me and Bumblebee can go head on and fry these fish and cook these beans."

Chapter 3

The Healer

Celeste

The doctor told my grandfather that he has prostate cancer. It is in its last stages. He doesn't have long to live. How will Maymay raise us four children and babysit T-Red and Bumblebee's children while caring for my sick granddaddy?

After she finds out that he has cancer and only a couple of months to live, she spends each day with him like it's their last day.

"Maymay, you gon' have to decide what y'all gon' do about burying me," T-Man says. Maymay knows that buying a tomb costs a lot of money, and they don't have much of an insurance policy. Many of her family members are just placed in the tombs with the other family members. Maymay knows she will have to make some hard decisions.

She has time to try to get her money together to pay for a tomb. She will also be looking for her own final resting place. She will engrave both of their names on the tomb before T-Man dies so that he can see her love for him. Bumblebee knows a lot of good people who want to help, so she decides to have a dinner.

Maymay's cousins serve the food. Unlike our family, they can pass for a white family, and many people wonder who the white people serving the food are. Bumblebee tells those who ask, "They are Maymay's high yellow cousins. They pass for white. You call that *passé blanc*. They don't associate with those who marry dark people, like me." She says it loud enough so that they can hear.

Maymay and T-Man are fair-skinned, but Mama and T-Red's children are darker than Maymay, because Mama had babies for dark men. T-Red's wife Bumblebee is also dark. Although Maymay's people from St. Martinville visit for weddings and funerals, they rarely visit for any other reason.

"Her family doesn't want to be white, but they do not want to be black, either. They are poor Mulattos who fish for a living. They are like us—poor," Bumblebee tells me.

"A lot of people showed up to support T-Man," Maymay says.

Yankee Doodle, the town drunk, has six plates from people who bought dinners but didn't want to eat them. He sits with his legs crossed like a child at the front of the door and eats his dinners hungrily as they continue to pile up. The food drips from his scraggly beard. When he is done, he goes into the burlap sack attached to the handlebar of his old, red, English racer bike. He says, "Mr. Yankee Doodle, would you like a sip of whisky? Don't mind if I do. Thank you very much, sir."

Mr. Yankee Doodle always talks to himself that way. When he has had enough to eat, he takes the remaining plates and stacks them in the front basket of his rusty, red bike and rolls away in his usual wobbly way on the side of the gravel shoulder of the narrow street.

We raise enough money to buy T-Man the tomb that he and Maymay would share. "People will help you in this town, no matter who you are. It's the good way of the people of Belle Place. People's moral conscience lead them to do what is right," Father Etienne tells the children as they look toward Yankee Doodle, who rides away, struggling to keep the dinners from falling from his basket.

Chapter 4

T-Red and Bumblebee

Bumblebee

I am Bumblebee. I am Maymay and T-Man only daughter-in- law. I lives further down the street, about forty feet away from Maymay and T-Man. T-Man and Maymay let me and Red park our trailer house on they property. They raised a lot of hell. They wanted to make sure we had our trailer paid off before we parked it in they li'l yard. They didn't want a bank to take their land if we owed on a trailer.

I work two jobs to make sure it is paid off. It didn't cost that much on account of it's used. It's old and rusty, but everybody come in it think it was bought new. Red so handy. He can fix anything. He a self-made carpenter, an electrician, and a plumber, and I am clean just like Maymay, except Maymay let her children be trifling and dirty. They work that poor woman like a dog.

Maymay starts calling my man "T-Red" after he meets me at the Sugar cane Festival and we start courting. Red so stupid. He think she call him that all of a sudden because he red and light-skinned, or high yeller, is what some people calls it. Other people calls it *passé blanc*. People got different names for it, but it all mean the same thing: light-skinned.

I know why that skinny, old bitch call my man "T-Red." I call her a bitch behind her back because she so prejudice and evil. She just like a white person, but she don't want to be white. She don't want to be black, either. She call herself Mulatto. People don't even use that word like they used to.

She call him "T-Red" 'cause she *think* I put something in his spaghetti sauce. That ingredient is too nasty to repeat. Use your imagination. She don't say it to my face, but she told her *passé blanc* family from St. Martinville that I am a hoodoo queen. She don't understand how a heavy-set black woman like me can marry a fine and handsome *passé blanc* man like Red.

She upset 'cause her family from St. Martinville don't like me. People from town tell me that Maymay talk about me to the few friends she got in Belle Place. She call me a big black gorilla. She say she don't like me 'cause I fool with hoodoo. I heard about the red tea before. I have relatives who do all kinds of hoodoo. I don't. I prayed for a good man, and God gave me Red, my trailer, and my children right next to her, and she gonna have to live with it and me, one way or the other.

Red tells me that she goes as far as getting her husband T-Man to pray on him so that he lose the hoodoo hex. Red tell them no, and he don't have time for that. He got four children from me, and he would never leave his children for no one. As religious as Maymay is, she wants me to divorce my old man. She say Father would okay the divorce because Red married me because of hoodoo.

Before I was married to Red, she would talk about me in front of my face like I was nobody, like I was just some old work boot or tree. When Red and me would be courting under the tree, she would sit about six feet away from us and tell T-Man right in front of me as loud as she could, "Why does T-Red like that woman so much? I've seen some women in Lawtell with big, thick, long plaits in they head following him at the Mardi Gras parade. They make him fig pie and boudin. They're so pretty and nice. They have nice shapes. He wants to bring this big, fat black woman to ma house."

She says that right in front of me. She roll her eyes and everything. Red would tell me all of the time to ignore her, and that's just what I did because I was always taught to respect my elders.

Well, it's so funny 'cause everything backfired. The more T-Man prayed on Red, the more he liked me and didn't like those high yeller girls. Most of them come from towns with other high yeller girls, like Maymay. They from small towns you miss if you blink your eyes.

Maymay come from a town that would run a dark man out with a gun if he would try to court one of them high yeller girls. They don't like black or white people in those towns. Red liked my cooking a lot, and he don't eat from anybody. He picky. He knows I am so clean. He likes to eat after clean people like his mama.

Maymay would be conniving and get those high yeller women to make him some dishes. When other women would give him food, he would say the pies are too sweet and the boudin is too greasy. He ain't never ate nothing them other women cooked him. He pitched it right there in the trash barrel and burnt it.

Since Red told me what Maymay was doing behind my back, I always made it a point to bring him food just so I could see the look on her face when he eat it in front of her.

I bring him a hot plate like red beans and pickle tips, fried chicken, okra gumbo, boudin, or crackling. When Maymay couldn't explain it any other way besides the hoodoo, she said I found the way to her son's heart through his stomach. We got married in the Catholic Church, and we had three beautiful children. Then when it came time to have my last child, he turned out to be a little mongoloid. The doctors call it down syndrome, but me and my family calls it mongoloid. Maymay calls him a little *bitie*. That's some Creole word I don't know.

I couldn't understand that, 'cause I thought that only old women had mongoloids. I was eighteen when I started having my children. Red and me got married straight out of high school. I was a virgin and so was Red. Everything about our marriage was perfect and holy.

Then I got to looking at T-Man and his healing he was doing next to us. As he praying on people, he shaking the sickness off his hands and on the ground. He heal people all the time on his property. I believe that somebody demons got in my belly, and I found out that even Father come to T-Man to get healed.

After I had my baby, I started going to a sanctified church because my own priest was dabbling in this foolishness. Tut has sex with every Tom, Dick, and Harry in Belle Place. Maymay is plain-as-day crazy. She believe there are men who hide in the sugar cane fields called Black Fuckers who are trying to rape all the grown women. The crazy part about it is Red believe it, and I don't know if T-Man believe it or not 'cause the man never talks. You would swear he mute.

This family is crazy. I tell you, crazy and cursed. I have a mongoloid child that look white. He has blond hair and blue eyes. That's crazy too, because I am blacker than a cast iron skillet.

Maymay is sitting under the tree. I tell her, "I brought y'all some food. I hope you like it." I carry two brown china plates wrapped in aluminum foil. "I only brought enough for you and T-Man. The rest of them know how to cook. I'm not slaving over a hot stove for none of them. They young, they can work. Too damn lazy, though. I'm talking 'bout Tut," I tell Celeste and Maymay. Celeste is sitting next to Maymay. Celeste is the only one who has a little sense. At least she tries to clean up. She ain't dirty and trifling like that gal, Tut. I say, "Don't worry, Celeste. I'm not talking about you."

I tell Maymay, "As soon as Red go in town and get the fat, I'm gon' make some hog cracklin's for T-Man. He say he may as well eat like he wants to. He's on his last leg," I say.

I look at Maymay's ashy and muddy feet. "Maymay, what I tell you about going in that garden with your bare feet. You gon' get the ringworm. You remember how Tut daughter got that plant in her leg, and it started growing all over her body? You better be careful. They have weird stuff out here in these demonic fields of sugar cane." I get the hose and begin to help Maymay wash the dry mud from her feet.

Maymay says, "I'm trying to take it all in. I never had anyone die close to me this way, somebody so good, like T-Man. I know it gon' rain when he die. Every time somebody good die, it storms. I see them dark clouds over yonder coming. He at the hour of his death."

I tell her, "I'm always going be here for Red and my family." I think that Maymay regrets how she used to treat me when I was young. She look at me like she knows I am telling the truth.

"I bring blessings wherever I go. I know if I'm going to be there for my husband, I'm going to be there for you. We've been going out since I was sixteen. I kept myself for him. I ain't never been with nobody else," I say. "You know what they say. When one die, another one coming. Somebody's going to come to take T-Man place. That is the circle of life, Maymay. One go, another one coming. Life changes with new and old."

Chapter 5

At the Hour of Our Death, Amen

Celeste

This is how my grandpa wanted to meet the Blessed Mother, at his house with all his children and grandchildren. We are all around him and Maymay's bed on our knees praying with our prayer beads. The rain pounds on the tin roof.

He tells Maymay, "You done been with me all these years, Maymay. We come to this place together. I want to leave this place on ma property with you by ma side. Everybody got to go, one day. I believe it's ma time. I want to see ma house and all the times we had together and look at the memories in the pictures. Take care of the chillen' and grandchillen'. I know you gon' do the best you can without me."

I know what this time means. He is holding on to her and the past memories.

They held each of their newborns in the same bed he rests in today, and we see them now with no more living left to do together.

"We had a good life together, you and me," Maymay tells Grandpa. She looks at him with those beautiful eyes that haven't changed like her old, wrinkled skin.

He tells Maymay in Creole, "*Na Ah Pee Tah.*" I will see you later. My grandpa never believed in the word "goodbye." He wants her to believe him. I think we all believe him. He takes his place in the sky.

Chapter 6

Soft Winds in the Belle Place Sky

Celeste

Every Sunday morning after the church congregation repeats Father's words, "Peace be with you," Maymay and I kindly offer our peace to those around us and exit the huge wooden doors; she tries not to stay long and have to entertain conversations about T-Man or Mama.

"T-Man's death check is here," I tell Maymay one day, holding a handful of mail. The Union National man had it mailed to us. Maymay says that it didn't take long at all.

Maymay says, "I know they was going to mail it on time, 'cause I always paid my bill on time." She keeps the policy envelope nailed to the wall in her tiny bedroom.

Bumblebee says, "You and T-Man always been like them poor people that be on TV. They give them a whole lot of money and they waste it all on junk food and stupid stuff."

Well, Maymay is spending her money on junk food today at LeBlanc's grocery with me. She paid for the tomb and the funeral, and now she has some money left over—not much. As T-Red waits outside in his car, Maymay listens to the women talking about Mama on aisle one. It is obvious that they want Maymay to hear them. Maymay thinks that they should have the decency to come to her and tell her, instead of being disrespectful to an old lady who has lost her husband a month ago.

"That's Tut's mama over there making groceries. You know Tut—the town ho. She tried to take Bo from Papoo. She told Papoo how much her man liked that crazy black juice that he always telling people Tut got. Papoo made her wish she never told her about it. She beat her on the side of this here store. She beat the mess out of that girl. I almost felt sorry for her, until I realized who she is. That girl think 'cause she red and look like a white girl that she can take all our mens. Nobody wants her. They just want to mess with her." The girls speak directly to Maymay now, as they look at her. Maymay doesn't ignore them. She stares right back at them.

T-Red says we have different daddies and he can't study about it, because it would be a whole other job to find out who our daddies are. We are definitely for Tut because we came out of her. Tut can say we for a man, but she has to prove it. We have each other, and that's enough. Our daddies came into our mama's life like the soft winds in the Belle Place sky.

Chapter 7

Mom Dot's Unnatural Sky

Celeste

Mom Dot lives where trees cover the sky. You look up and all you see are trees, moss, and birds. I am used to open spaces, running through the fields on dirt roads under the wide and very blue sky, but Mom Dot's house has trees covering the sky. I feel like I'm in another world, and it is so scary.

Mom Dot, Bumblebee's aunt, sees things through people and dreams. She has been known to tell Maymay things that mysteriously happen in the future. She is a *traiteur* like my grandpa and a tea woman. She is Maymay's lifelong friend. Maymay wants to know what is going to become of Tut, so she visits Mom Dot.

Mom Dot is seventy years old, but she looks so much younger. She has silky brown skin and a kind face. She is a Creole-speaking woman who always wears a head scarf on her head that matches one of the several straight cotton dresses she calls banana dresses.

Her property sits along the Bayou Teche. A rickety picket fence that was never painted white surrounds her house. To get to her house, you have to drive through the huge trees that look tangled in the sky.

Her front yard is a rainbow of colorful flowers, and I don't know how they grow with so little sunlight. She lives in a slave cabin. No one wants to call it a slave cabin, but that's what it is. I read books about them, and I've visited plantations for field trips. It's a cypress house with two side-by-side doors. She has a lot of nice colorful lilies, daffodils, and sunflowers. She also has electricity and running water in that cabin. Every time I visit her, I never want to touch anything. As much as I love dogs, I avoid the mixed beagle that smiles below me. I dare not touch her dog.

Mom Dot screams at the dog, "Come back, ya." She is half blind, so she has to wait until T-Red introduces himself. She doesn't know who her dog is playfully barking at.

"Hey Mom Dot, it's Red, Maymay, and her granddaughter. We come here to ask a favor," T-Red yells as all of us approach her.

"What's that y'all say?" Mom Dot asks as she looks in the direction of his voice.

"I'll let Maymay explain," T-Red says.

Maymay passes through a gathering of brown hens in the yard. She tells T-Red to place them in the wooden chicken coup.

"Well, y'all come in. I fixed some beef tripe and turnip greens. Ya'll are welcome to some." No matter what's cooked in the pot, people always offer us something to eat when we visit.

"No thanks. Maybe later. We just ate some boudin and crackling," Maymay says, approaching the porch.

Maymay steps over a pregnant cat's tail, and it hisses and scratches her. "*Iyiyi*," screams Maymay.

"That cat is crazy. I ought to drown her in that there bayou. Last time she was pregnant, she went under them steps and ate all of them baby kittens. It made ma *grandbebe* cry for two days. It happens like that, sometimes. I don't like to kill ma animals, but I've got to kill her. Those babies are going to die a terrible death. You know animals go crazy just like people, they say. At least that's what they say," Mom Dot says.

"I see that you must have about thirty cats running around here," Maymay looks around her. There are cats sitting on an old car. There are cats sitting on the porch swing, sitting in the window, and walking through the yard.

"You have a lot of trees. It's so nice and peaceful. I like coming to your house, Mom Dot. I like the peaceful feeling. I only got one big oak tree on ma property and some trees in the woods past the fields. I love ma old oak tree," Maymay asks. "What you doing with all these cats, Mom Dot?"

"They keep the field mice away, and they keep me company. It's hard to get cats now-a-days. People don't give them away. I don't give away none of ma cats. People too mean to the animals around ya. Ma neighbor takes his and slams them against the trees and kills them. They be havin' blood on the tree trunks. He is so crazy, that there boy. They don't like all of them animals in they yard. I seen him drown them one by one in the duck pond, while the little boy who lives there cry and cry. He go outside and just swing and swing, all day. Maybe people getting like me and don't want to see they animals hurt. People mean now days, Maymay. They not like you and me. We give people anything and help everybody, but not them, *non*. Not them," Mom Dot says. She holds the cat in her arms.

Maymay begins to cry. "Yes, Mom Dot people are so mean, now days. It is a new kind of mean. Cushma himself be riding down this bayou. I see him swinging through the trees."

I don't like when Maymay talks about Cushma. Cushma is a man devil that has sex with women while they are sleeping. He rides you. Maymay has many scary stories about him.

Mom Dot looks toward Maymay and says, almost in a whisper, "I had a dream last night, Maymay, and I know why you come."

Maymay says, "You just don't know, Mom Dot. You just don't know what I be going through around this place. I all the time thought that maybe Tut would slow down when T-Man passed away, but look like that fire her up more. Look like that make her mo' crazy. All she cares about is twisting her ass around every man she sees. She wants to see what she can get for it."

"You come to find out why Tut is the talk of the town and why she be giving you so much trouble," Mom Dot tells Maymay.

"*Mais oui*, you know. You hear about her in the streets, don't you?" Maymay asks as she wipes her eyes.

"*Mais non, cher*. Don't doubt me. Listen good. I had a dream about Tut, and ma dream was made true by something I saw by ma house. You have to look for things that don't fit, Maymay, and that is how things get told to me," Mom Dot says as she looks at Maymay with sympathy.

"Mom Dot, I never doubt you. I know that through ma rosaries and novenas that God has nothing to do with this. This is the hand of the mean devil. Every time I've come here before, you always can tell me what's going on, because God is trying to tell me how to live ma life. But, I truly believe that Tut done sold her soul to the devil. How come I know? She tells me so herself," Maymay says as she settles in her chair.

"One day, she comes home at two in the morning. She pissy drunk. I tell her, 'You not coming in ma house. Leave!' She broke the window with a stick. There is glass all over her children. She coulda killed them. All I hear is crying and screaming.

"I'm too weak to stop her. I send Celeste for T-Red, who over there by his trailer. I tell Celeste to tell him to come and get Tut clean away from ma property. She done shattered glass all over her babies. He comes huffing and puffing, mad as a .45 gun. Mom Dot, he don't look it, but that boy can raise hell, yeah. He come and grab her by her big hair and throw her in the chicken coup. He says she ain't coming in nare-o-one of the houses. He don't want to kick her off ma property 'cause she would just get in more of a mess.

"He beat her real good. I don't have to get him a switch that time. And she deserved every lick. She selfish, her. She don't care about nobody but herself. She slept on the back porch with ma dogs. The next day, when she not drunk and helping me with work, I ask her how she can do such a thing. She tells me she sold her soul to the devil. She keeps saying it and sweeping and laughing. How come I know she serious is, she's not drunk. She tells me she done talked to him, and he says he would take her soul for three bottles of whiskey and to be young and pretty all her life. She says she gave Cushma her soul and some hot Creole sex. She says she never want to be old and wrinkled, like me. Cushma owns her. She belongs to that sex devil," Maymay shouts.

"Do you remember your last time you came here, Maymay?" Mom Dot asks.

"Yeah, you gave me some holy water to put under ma porch because Nitah was trying to steal ma T-Man. You told me never let a woman in ma house, because she can put hoodoo in ma house." Maymay says.

"A month after I put that stuff under ma porch, T-man tells me that for sure she is after him. I always wonder why that holy water never cured Tut, though. That sex devil still not dead. Once you sell your soul to the devil, God don't want nothing to do with you. T-Red says Bumblebee showed him where it is in her big letter *Bible*," Maymay says.

"Let me tell you," Mom Dot says.

"Go head, tell me!" says Maymay.

"Well, I went to sleep early last night. I went into ma peaceful sleep. I know what that sleep be. It be one of two things: either the Blessed Virgin Mary coming to me to give me a sign of what is to come, or it be the devil, Cushma, trying to trick me into believing his evilness," she says.

I look at her face, and I am so scared of her blind eye that is staring straight ahead. It is not supposed to be staring at me, but I feel that her eye has a mind of its own. It is looking at me. I think about Bumblebee, who always reminded my Maymay about Mom Dot's teas that pass babies. I think about that tea next to her holy water. I want to run, but I feel like the eye is hypnotizing me. It has me frozen.

"Yes, Maymay, the dead, the spirits, and the saints talk to me. They come to me while I be sleeping. I know a day or two after people die, just before the wakes and the blessings, they come to me. I can set a watch and clock to it. It is the Virgin Mary trying to speak to me and carry news back to the family, so y'all can pray for them in purgatory," Mom Dot kisses the Virgin Mary that she wears around her neck.

"You see, in ma dream, I see this light. I get closer and closer to the light and there's this house that I ain't never seen before. I feel like I can sit down and walk wherever I please. It is bigger than a church. In the house, there be this lady. She wearing a purple shirt with yellow flowers. She says, 'It hurts. It hurts.' I wake up the next day, and I see a blue bird. She watches over us, Maymay. She watches us. You see, it is the Virgin Mary trying to tell us to pray for Tut's spirit. You see? Now, if she sold her soul like you say, the Virgin Mary would not tell me to tell you to pray for her. You see? She got hope! You see?"

"Well, I'll be!" says Maymay "She has that purple shirt. *Mais*, I sewed it for her. There is no way that you could've know that. Them children lost it playing in the closet. She made a big fuss about it. I almost had to call the cops on ma property, that girl cut up so much for that shirt. You know what you talking about, Mom Dot," Maymay says.

Maymay sits in Mom Dot's little living room on the soft mattress. She is full hope now that she knows that Mama's soul does not belong to the devil. My eyes are now glued to that iron headboard that holds rosaries and holy leaves. She said that Cushma comes in her dreams. I want to know more about her talks with him and her evil cat.

On the wall is a picture of the Virgin Mary and a crucifix. Like Mom Dot, Maymay keeps the rosary and the cross near the bed. Whenever Cushma the demon tries to ride her while she is sleeping, she holds the rosary, and he moves into the wall like the smoke that rises from a trash pit.

"What do I got to do to bring her soul back?" Maymay asks.

"You need to pray for her, Maymay. You need to pray. She is messing with mean, devilish people who mean her harm. People are going to try to hurt her, but you got to be strong for her. You got to prop her up on every leaning side like the good Lord does for his children. Pray for her and listen to her. Help the poor child. He hurts too many people. He is evil. I always can sense evil, Maymay. Just like T-Man can feel the pain of those he done healed, I can feel when evil coming. I feel it coming like the sky feels the thunder. I know it like ma own back hand."

Maymay knows that many people know how to make others go crazy. That's why we burn our hair, and we don't give out pictures. Hoodoo people take your hair and pictures and make you go crazy. Maymay always flushes her hair down the toilet or burns it. No crazy spirits will come to us. I don't believe all of that stuff. I believe Mom Dot's blind eye, though.

Maymay left Mom Dot with a hug, a kiss, and five dollars of T-Man's death check money. Even though Mom Dot refused, Maymay tucked it into the pocket of her pretty banana dress. She tells her to buy some candles so that she can pray for Tut and her family. I wanted Maymay to give that money to me. I never get money for helping, and my sisters and me always need things.

"I want to eat," T-Red says, and Mom Dot is happy to serve Maymay and T-Red on the table in her middle room. Everything is so neat and clean. I sit on the floor, and the pregnant cat rubs against me. I do something that I normally don't do. I pet it. It seems so sweet. It is a yellow cat with thick fur. I don't sense anything evil about this cat. It looks fancier than the other cats.

Suddenly, I feel the eye. Mom Dot throws the five dollars next to the cat and hands me a brown burlap sack. She doesn't have to say anything to me. I wrap my two hands around the cat's belly. I can feel the babies moving. The cat doesn't make a sound. I tie a knot around the top of the sack, and I run through the beautiful flower garden of yellow, red, and purple flowers. I stop at the bayou. The cat is now moving, startled by my running. I throw the sack in the bayou. I don't want the babies to suffer. I don't want Mom Dot's blind eye to hear the babies scream when the mother decides to eat them. The sack goes down, and the cat screams as high as the oak trees that cover the sky.

When we leave, the little specks of blue sky above us darken as the sun is setting. Now, it seems like nighttime. When we get home, I take a bleach bath to wash away Mom Dot's bag and her unnatural sky.

Chapter 8

They Cuttin' and Burnin' Cane and the Ashes Rise to the Sky

Tut

The rooster crowing its ass off, and I want to sleep but it's food stamp day. I gotta get up before T-Red and Maymay start they shit. Speaking of shit, Celeste's cat is in the house letting me know it needs to go out. Celeste cat is the only one trained. Everything is perfect about her. She makes me sick.

Chat! You and the dogs are not allowed in here. I don't care what Maymay says about a potty-trained cat. I kiss the cat on the mouth. I'm going to clean these blue walls today.

They getting too dirty. Diana Ross pictures don't look good on dirty walls.

I don't need friends. All I need is my pigs, my angel pictures, my music, and my Diana Ross.

I dance to the music in my head and talk to myself.

I am a very talented woman.

Dear Diana,

Last night I hitched a train into town. I met a rich white man who wore an expensive suit. He thought that I was so beautiful. He looked at my body from head to toe and licked his thin lips right in front of me. He told me that there was something different about me, but he couldn't put his finger on it. He owns a carnival business, and he was hiring carnies for a fair in town. He wanted to take me out to a fancy restaurant, but I told him that I was colored, and we could stop the small talk if he just would give me a 100 bucks. That's how much it costs at those restaurants anyway. Maymay always tell me to tell white men that I am *colored, because I can get in trouble like that movie Imiatation to Life. We watch it every time it come on. Maybe I won't get lynched, but I can get raped and left for dead. He looked at me different when I told him I was colored. He told me that he don't know what it is about Mulattos, but they always fascinated him. We had sex in the back of his white Lincoln Continental on the red leather seat. He gave me $100, and he used a condom. I told him that it's too bad that we can't keep a business relationship, but I told him that I would look out for him when the next carnival rolls into town. I would look past the fields for the lights. And just think, Maymay say that I can't keep up with who I have sex with. It's all between you and me, Diana. It's here in my hoe book.*

Love, TUT

I place the diary on my chifferobe next to the picture of Diana Ross. It's the one with her neck held back, and she is smiling with her hair all tangled and wild. Papoo and the card players say that's the one that look like me the most.

It is grinding time. It's starting to get cool. Soon they'll be harvesting the cane, and I will lose my little room there. I'll keep it for as long as I can. I'm going to go out now and tend to the animals, I tell Diana Ross.

Hey y'all missed me? I ask the pigs. They rush over to where I stand. I pet them one by one on the head. I don't like neat, potty-trained cats as much as I like sweet, fat pigs. I don't have to pretend. They listen. I pet them one by one.

Don't get too big, now. T-Red is going to put a knife to your throats. I pretend to slice my throat. They are smart. They don't smile with T-Red or run to the fence when he come by them.

I now move over to the chicken coup to feed the chickens.

Y'all are the nastiest animals on earth. Y'all eat anything, even your own poop.

I can see the men working in the fields, harvesting the cane. Soon, I'll be able to see the highway again. I stare at them, but I don't bother telling them hi. T-Red has schooled all of the men about me.

I have a simple cotton flower sundress on that Maymay sewed for me with cheap, leftover fabric. Maymay always sew until all of the material is gone. She sew underwear, bras, and purses. The dress is yellow with little pink flowers. I didn't bother to comb my hair this morning.

It is check day, and Maymay is going to buy everything on my list if I do all of her work.

After slopping the hogs and feeding the chickens, I start hanging clothes. I try to hang the clothes without falling asleep. The white sheets smell like fresh detergent. I just want to close my eyes and sniff them.

As I struggle to stay awake, I glance at the men who have begun their morning job of cutting cane. Out there is someone I never seen before. He is a handsome, dark man on the tractor. He see me and wave. I see him looking and liking what he see. I like what I see.

He has muscles and drives the tractor like a Cadillac. He gets closer, and I get hotter and hotter by this dark man I never seen on the tractors before. I know all of the other men, and they know me, all too well. I can't move. I just stare as he come in my space. I move away from the white sheet and I look at him long and hard. The mosquitoes are biting, and it feels like a million needles sticking me. Something about this morning don't seem right.

I lift my dress and slap them away, almost forgetting the stranger who is looking at me and my long legs covered in dew and blood from the ten or so dead mosquitoes. I move to the handsome stranger on the tractor. The sun gettin' higher in the sky, and my matching panties and bra shows through the light cotton dress. I feel hot and sticky, like the morning. Something about this man working make me even hotter.

His nice calming voice is the only one I hear this morning. His face is so close and beautiful now.

"Hey little red," he says, "*Quest ton nom*?"

"What did you say?' I say.

"Do you speak French?" he asks.

"No!" I say. "My Maymay do, but I don't. All I know is English. Where are you from?"

"I'm from Sunset," he say.

"My mama say they speak a lot of French there. They even teach it to their children. What your name?"

"My name Black. What's yours?"

"My name Theresa, but they calls me Tut," I say.

"Well, Tut, you ever rode a tractor before?" he ask me.

"Hell, I've rode everything in these fields from big tractors to big … use your imagination, handsome."

"Your skin is so pretty and clear, it looks like a baby behind," Black say. "What do you use on your skin?"

"Every night, I wash my face with hot water from the tea kettle and Ivory soap," I say.

"You smell like these black woods, sweaty and wild with a little sweetness," Black say softly, almost as though he don't want me to hear. Men don't usually speak like this around here. They get straight to the point and straight to the ass.

"How long have you been working these fields? I haven't seen you before," I say as I cover my eyes from the sun and look at him.

"I come out here to help my uncle out. Things kind of slow where I'm at. I usually work in the potato fields. The harvest wasn't too good last year. I fix cars part time and work in the fields the other time," Black say.

"You got a girlfriend out there in Sunset?" I ask.

"Not as pretty as you." Black look at me from my muddy flip-flop feet to my hair. His eyes make their way up my body nice and slow, like he is ironing my body with eyes. He look at me as if he is searching for something beyond the raggedy cotton dress that I wear. I like his slow and not hurrying way.

This bra that I wear is so loose that my breasts are now bare, and the cheap dollar store material is balled up under and around my big hard nipples. Why should I act anything but who I am, even though this moment and this man are unlike anything in Belle Place.

"You just saying that I'm pretty and sweet 'cause you want to smell my panties. All mens start off with compliments, then they move on to the bed." I straighten my panties and dig in for my bra and cover my nipples, all while he looks. He get a glance of my big, round nipples, and he clear his throat.

"What you do out there in the country Frenchy town of Sunset?" I ask.

"I go to a lot of trail rides. I like riding through the fields like this. Belle Place has a lot of nice places for trail rides. It is nice, back here. You like these fields?" ask Black.

"I like messing around in the fields. They don't call them headlands for nothing." I wink at Black. "Take me for a ride out there with you in the fields," I say.

He is wearing a clean, white wife-beater. It look even whiter than most next to his dark chocolate skin.

"You bring me back before noon, or else my Maymay come hunt me down through the cane, holding a switch in her hand. She gon' have my ass out there in the fields."

Black gets down and picks me up with his strong muscular arms. He plops me on the seat. He sit in front of me and crank up the tractor, and I wrap my skinny arms around Black's smooth stomach. As the ride gets bumpy, I hold on to his leather belt and his navy blue work pants. I kick off my flip-flops and smooth my bare feet over his hard steel-toe boots, now gritty with dirt. I grind my feet against his boots. He smell like diesel and freshly plowed dirt as we ride through the fields.

"You're something else, girl. You have the dirtiest mouth on the prettiest face," Black say, as he tries to steer the tractor with one hand and hold on to me with the other.

"Well, I'm just an old country girl, never been too much of anywhere but these ya silly fields," While I am talking, I'm trying not to get tossed over. I love the way the wind feel in my hair. I guess the dust will stick to my hair like the dust on Maymay's yellow and white chickens.

"I like me some trail rides and some *bouchieries* and Craklin fair. That's all they have here in Belle Place—nothing more. One day, I want to go somewhere big like Motown. I always wanted to find and beat that bitch Diana Ross's ass for stealing my songs," I tell Black. I see that he don't like the wet screaming that I'm doing in his ear.

He say, "What's that you say?"

"Yeah, you heard me right. The bitch stole my songs. I let her get away with 'Endless Love' and 'Upside Down,' but she keep taking them. I am the first one to sing 'Upside Down You Turning Me' and all of that. My song is still in my Big Chief tablet. I can show you—it's dated and everything. I don't know how she's getting them. The tablet is hid and everything. My brother T-Red tells me I got to do a poor man's copyright. He's tired of me saying the same thing over and over. He say if I keep saying it, he is going to get Bumblebee, his old woman, to beat me up. He even gave me the papers to fill out for the certified mail, but I lost them like five times."

His look toward me changes, and he just laughs. I look back, and Maymay's house gets further and further away. I know that I shouldn't be out in the fields playing around. There is so much to do back home. I have to make the beds, cook the dinner, and clean the children's room.

We ride through the fields on this, our day we stole. This day feel like my day. It's my day and Black day. We done stole a day. The other men pay little attention to us. Another driver uses a parked tractor and takes Black's place in the fields. Two hours pass. We talk about so many things. Black is a joker that makes me laugh louder than I have ever laughed in a long time.

The day is bright and quiet. It's just the big blue sky and the sugarcane and me and Black. No Maymay. No children. No T-Red. Rain is coming from the east. That big blue sky start to bark and yell at me and Black for taking this our day away. Lightening shoots from the sky, and the thunder is talking to us.

We not scared, as the dark skies now chase us through the sugarcane. That sky done sent little winds and dust tornadoes and the smell of fresh rain to follow us and end our day, but all I want to do is have fun before the rain comes.

"Look at the sky over there. It's got sun and rain. My friend Papoo tells me that mean the devil beating his wife. That is what happens when you have one part of the sky filled with rain and the other with sunshine. The devil be beating his wife," I say.

"What do you do out here during the day?" Black asks.

"Well, I look out for the Black Fuckers, that's for sure."

"What?" he asks.

"Maymay says there are Black Fuckers out in this sugar cane. She's seen them herself. They are black men who are trying to get her and rape her, me, and her granddaughters. They were also trying to break her and T-Man up, because they jealous of their long relationship when he was alive. They work with a woman, the Big Bitch. It's just one woman. She really hates Maymay. She's her enemy. She used to shine a light at night while Maymay and T-Man, my daddy, was sleeping. She wanted to catch them having sex and stop them by shining a light on them. Now, T-Man dead, so the Big Bitch is just working with them to drive Maymay crazy and torment her about T-Man's death. Everybody knows that—even T-Red. He has the most sense out of everybody."

"Do you really believe that?" asks Black.

"If my Maymay says it, I know it is the truth. Why wouldn't it be? Why would she lie on a thing like that? When you live back here in the middle of cane fields, you see all kinds of stuff. People hunt in there and do all kinds of stuff—even cheat on they wives and husbands in the headlands. You never know what's happening. Maymay see people moving and running in here all the time," I say.

"I get so lonely in the day time. That house looks like an ant back there. I wish that I could ride far, far away until it's just a dot that I cannot see anymore. I would need one of those microscopes at my daughter Celeste's school to see it, and even then, I would laugh because it too small to touch, to smell, or to hear. I'm tired of minding children all day and working. I want fun like everyone else. I am tired of sharing Maymay and T-Man's dream of the house with a doorbell on the bedroom door and a screened back porch. I want my own house and my own dreams where I can live and run with my hair loose in my own bunch of sugar cane with someone who make me laugh all day like you. This is my first time riding a tractor through the fields. It's so much fun," I say.

"You smell like a strong man. When I was young, I used to comb my daddy, T-Man's hair. He smelled sweaty and strong. I like that smell. You have it, but it's different. I just want to stick to you like a puppy to its mamma's tit." I wrap my arms around Black's muscular chest. I press my face on his dark, sweaty back.

"I want to show you something. Stop the tractor right here."

Black stops the tractor and jumps off of it to gently help me down.

"It is somewhere here." I turn around and around like a crazy dog chasing its tail. "You see that tree there in the middle of the field?" I ask. I point to the tree yonder in the field.

"Yeah, what about it?" say Black.

"That's our secret tree me and my brothers had when we were young. When we was young, we went there and started a club. After we drank Kool-Aid and ate cookies, we made an oath to always be there for each other. They probably forgot. T-Red the only one of my brothers left, and he don't talk about it anymore, but I remember. Only I did something special. Come see," I say.

"Do you see that big red ribbon that is tied on the top of that stalk? I have my own room there. I go there to get away from everyone." We walk ten feet deep into the sugar cane. I see the red ribbon that mark my spot. The cane is high and ready to be harvested. It grow above our heads. The sky know that we need the rain. I love the way cracked dirt feel on my soft, bare feet. The tall, straight stalks cut our skin like a thousand paper cuts across our bodies. I feel Black's fear. He probably think that I am going to kill him and leave him for the wild animals.

"Wait. You have to take an oath with me. The oath say that you will never reveal the secret spot to anyone."

He say, "I promise I won't reveal the secret spot to anyone." Once he has promised to keep the secret, I pull him into my homemade room.

My room look like a little grass hut with no ceiling—only the blue sky.

"In all my years of cutting cane, I ain't seen nothing like this," Black say. "I guess if you a lonely country girl, you do what you need to pass the time. I just don't know why I kept following you. Maybe I couldn't stop following that wild pretty hair. Maybe I couldn't stop looking at that goofy cotton dress with the matching panties and bra. I don't even know if this day is real."

"This is where I come to rest my mind during the day when the children at school and all my chores are done. I love it. I think that maybe my Maymay is seeing Cushma in the fields, and she think that they are the men who are trying to rape us. Bully, my cousin, tell me that Cushma is a succubus. He have sex with women. There is a name for the one that has sex with the men, but I don't know it. I always ask my sister Bumblebee. She tells me all the time, but I forget."

"This is very strange, Theresa. Your eyes look wild now. Your looks are changing just like the sky roof of this house." We both look at the sky that was once blue. It is dark now.

"Don't you worry about getting hurt out here? An attractive girl like you can really get hurt," Black say as he look around the little cane room. For the first time, he worried about me. He not laughing no more and chasing me in the ripe cane.

"I don't worry about it much. I come out here and relax and look at my dream books. I write in my tablets, sing, or do whatever I want. It get hard, always hearing people talk bad about me because, as Maymay say, I made too many mistakes in life. She say a girl with all my mistakes and children will never be able to make it in this world," I say.

"Well, there are coons and possums and wild dogs and big cats out here in these fields. I know because I clear them out of here and see them when I'm riding on my tractor," Black says

"I don't care. I need my own room. I don't have no place back there in the big house. I always had to share everything with my brothers, and now I have to share with my wild children. They break up everything. I can't have nothing to myself. I hide my soda and candy, and they always finding them. They eat and drink everything what belongs to me," I say.

I had a really nice purple shirt with yellow flowers that Maymay sewed for me to go to church. I can't find it, because those children always playing in my closet. The cat had its babies in my closet and messed up about ten of my outfits. I can't wash the blood out no matter how hard I try. Maymay taught me a prayer to say so that I could find the purple shirt: *Saint Anthony Saint Anthony, Something has been lost and can't be found, Can you please help me look around.*

I say that prayer every day for four months, and I still can't find my shirt. You know how you just feel good in some clothes? Well, I just felt so good in that shirt. I don't feel like Tut in that shirt.

Tut, who everybody hate, who everyone makes fun of. A white lady tell me I look like a yellow-headed Jaclyn Smith in that shirt. The teachers call me ma'am in that shirt.

"Be honest and tell me about everything you do when you come here in this place." Black says.

"I look at my magazines and dream. I write my songs, hoping that no one else will steal them, and I draw pictures. I really like to draw and paint. I hide all my stuff here in my own little box," I say.

I make sure that no one else but Black is listening or watching, and I lift a patch of sugar cane. I dig about fourteen inches deep and take out a rusty metal can. In the can is a red Big Chief tablet. I have my songs and magazines in this tablet to keep them safe from the rain. I take out two of my catalogs.

These are catalogs that come in the mail. This is the book that Maymay uses to buy stuff. I look at these and say, "I'm going to buy this or that." I love pretty clothes. I love looking in the windows when I go to town and say, "I'm going to get this or that." My daddy used to call me Pretty Clothes. I can't buy any of those clothes and things, so I just dream.

I have four children, and my Maymay tells me that I have to get stuff for my children before I get for me. She say that it is time that I stop acting young. Once you have children, your life is over and their life begin. My life been over since I was fourteen years old. Now, I am still young, but I have children. I can't go to college like people I know or get a job in town working at those pretty clothes shops. I just got to think about it. One day, my children will grow up, and I can go to Motown and sing my songs or work in a pretty clothes shop, but I'll probably be forty, and they don't have too many people that age living they dreams.

I have one smart girl. Her name is Celeste. She is so pretty and smart. She growing up, and soon she will be a woman like me. Maymay don't want her to end up like me. She got all kinds of dreams for that gal. She gonna make the family look good again because all the teachers and everybody at the school like her. She know more than anybody in her catechism class 'cause she all the time reading Bumblebee big letter *Bible*. All she want to do is read books and the *Bible*. She not gonna be like me. Black listens to every word.

Then, there is Tiny; she is sassy and lazy. That girl there gives me so many problems. I be whipping her all the time, and it still don't help. I have twins Hattie and Mattie. They are just normal little children who are pretty much raising theyselves. They rock theyselves to sleep, get their own food, and watch TV. I have to watch T-Red four children all the time. He lives next to my mama.

"You sure do talk a lot. You go on and on and don't stop," he laughs.

"I'm not used to people listening to me. They always be fussing about me or at me. They never listen to me. It's nice to have someone who can listen for a little while." I give Black a sweet, dimpled smile. He is sitting next to me on the mashed sugar cane and begins looking at the magazines and the artwork.

"What is this?" he ask me as he holds up my sketchpad.

"It's an angel. I love to draw angels," I say. "One day before you leave, I'll draw you an angel." Black looks at me and smiles. He thinks that I am really sweet—strange but sweet.

He sees my private stuff that no one knows about. He is special.

"Everybody is always telling me to do stuff. I never have time to hear myself think. I come here to get away sometimes," I say.

All of a sudden, small drops of rain begin to drip drop, and make little puddles on the sugar cane leaves. The wind and the rain begin to sweep through the sugar cane slowly, then faster.

"Let me put my stuff up," I say. I put everything where it belong.

Black carries me through the sugar cane field like the big strong fine man he is. He cover my face with his strong, big arms, and he take all of the paper cuts for me by covering my face and arms with his huge dark arms. He run as quickly as he can through the row of high, tangled sugar cane and put me on the tractor.

The rain now stings our bodies, and the house gets closer and closer, as both of us are silent because we know our stolen day is over. Black stops the tractor on the headland in front of my house. I jump off of the tractor and run for the porch. I stand on the porch, turn around, and look at him for the last time.

He want me to invite him in. I can tell. The moment is as quiet and as long as time and that mean sky will let it to be. The mud is on my body like cake batter. Muddy water drips from my body onto the clean porch. My cotton smock don't hide none of my womanly secrets, as the wet dress show my big titties, my butt crack, and my coochie. My look of madness is gone. His look of fear is gone. I want his hard, steel toe boots under my soft, wet feet. I am muddy and pretty. He is wet and handsome.

We both steaming like that hot tin roof now that the cool waters soothe the baking metal. He licks the muddy water from his sweaty, full lips as he sit on the tractor with his white wife beater clinging to his wet body showing his manhood. He wave and give me a smile, revealing all of his white, straight teeth. We know what we want, but as hot as I am, I know better than to mess with Maymay's house. She would kill me dead with her shotgun

"Maymay don't want nobody in her house. I would invite you in, but this is not my house," I say and my voice grows into a yell as the rain wails louder. "I'll see you tomorrow," I yell at him through the thunder and lightning. I turn around and splash water over the dry porch that is getting wetter by the moment. I run barefoot through the house, and the door slams behind me.

I close the windows. My feet leave muddy footprints. I forgot about the baking chicken in the oven that Maymay told me to watch. Outside the back door, I can see that the three lines of clothes that I hung together are now soaking wet.

I begin to do as much as I possibly can. I take the chicken out of the oven and place it in the white slop bucket on the back porch. The okra is no good and burnt. The children will have nothing to eat and no clean clothes to wear tomorrow to school.

I know that I stole this day, and I am ready to face my punishment. I look like something the dogs dragged in from the swamps. I don't want to look like this when Maymay gets home.

When Black comes tomorrow, I'll cook him some pecan candy. T-Red says I make the best pecan candy and red Kool-Aid.

I comb my sticky tangles out of my hair. The tea kettle is whistling, first softly then loudly. I run wet and naked through the kitchen to get it. The scalding water spills on my wrist and burns like a hot iron. I pour water in the foot tub, and I wash myself off.

Black didn't seem to mind that I was dirty. He just wanted to stare at me and lick his lips. He was as dirty as me. We both looked like children, today. I wet the towel in the warm, soapy water and rub my muddy arms and skin. My naked body is clean again.

I look at my dry belly. It is still flat, even after four children. Will Mr. Black put another child in my belly? Will I finally love having a baby? I never liked having those other babies. They were all curses that I didn't want. Maymay said they were innocent. I don't know if I ever really loved them, but I want to have a baby growing inside of me for a man like Black.

I hear T-Red's Nova splashing in the yard. "Oh, shit!" I say.

Two doors slam, and I hear Maymay's voice. "Go tell Tut to help me get these groceries from the car," she tells T-Red.

"Tut!" T-Red screams as he walks through the house. I am putting on a clean pink housedress.

"Open this damn door, Tut," he yells. I open the door. Maymay is already fussing about all them damn clothes still on the line. "You better get ready girl," T-Red tells me. He knows that any minute Maymay is going to walk in fussing. Maymay runs in from the rain with three bags of groceries.

"*Non, non*, I know dis is not my house looking like dis. I'll be damn. Come out here and help me get these damn groceries before I rawhide your ass with a leather strap."

I grab as many bags as I can and place them on the front porch. Soon, all the bags are in the kitchen.

T-Red says, "You know, Maymay I don't care. Even though that bitch is old, I could still whip her ass. I'm starting to see what you mean. Nothing about Tut makes an ounce of sense. Hard like Bumblebee, you, and me work to make ends meet for everybody don't matter to her. She up in here washing her pretty white girl hair instead of cooking for the children. I would beat that bitch ass, I tell you. Get T-man's black and white belt with the stars. Get it from that nail and wear that bitch out. We keep that belt on the nail for the kids, and that is just what she is. I can't go nowhere without them men telling me what a slut that gal is. Wear that bitch out. Wear her out, I tell you. This gal got you seeking spirits to see what's wrong with her. Bumblebee holding prayer groups behind Tut to pray that she finds God. It's too much."

Maymay says, "I done changed my mind. No matter what you say, Tut too old for a whipping. What would her children say if we whip her? She is just like a child, but we don't have to treat her like one. We'll end up whipping her until she is fifty. It's gon' play out one of these days. That ho-ing gon' play out. She must have been ho-ing or doing something she ain't got business." I can hear them from the car. They talk about me as if I am not there. I walk in with the last bag of groceries and a jug of Borden's milk.

Maymay says, "Look at ma house! Where you been at?"

T-Red says, "Remember them niggers been working out in the fields clearing them up. She probably is in ya house messing around with one of 'em," T-Red says.

"Oh no, T-Red, don't tell me that. She know I don't let nobody in ma house," Maymay says.

"You being messy, T-Red. You know I don't play with Maymay house. I know better than that," I say. "I'll do everything, Maymay. Just wait. I'm going to take care of the animals and cook some spaghetti and meatballs. Mrs. Canoe will let me use her dryer. I'll use Celeste's money in the piggy bank to pay for the gas. I promise I'll do it all."

I pick up a box of cereal and place it in the pantry. I need to impress Maymay so that I can cook my pecan candy and make my red Kool-Aid for Black. Maybe one day, Black will take me away from Maymay and her mean thunder and lightning sky.

Chapter 9

Food Stamp Day

Celeste

"That's why yo' mama wear cowboy boots when she fools around with people husbands," Bobby yells at me from the back of the bus. "You're trying to be all high and mighty. We know who you are. I'm gonna get you in those fields. Be careful."

I ignore Bobby. He is the bus bully. He is scared of Liver, who is playing hooky from school today. He doesn't bully us when he is on the bus. I sit in the first seat always so that I don't have to see anyone—only the road ahead.

As the oldest, I watch out for my sisters, brothers, and little cousins like a mother hen.

There is no street sign on the road that leads to Maymay's house. You would never know that someone lived down the street from the black top road. The house looks like a grain of salt on the horizon. It is just a long gravel road that extends miles down the road, and then the dusty headlands lead you to the rows and rows of sugar cane. My four sisters and T-Red's gang are all that are left on the slow-moving bus 57.

We are hungry, and we know it is food stamp day, so we're excited to see what treats Maymay has bought for us. Maymay promised that she would buy pecans so that Mama could make pecan candy for everyone.

T-Red's younger children, Kojo and Meemee, run to the mud puddles in the yard. They begin to pretend that the puddle is a swimming pool. They splash through the puddles and laugh.

I am angry because I know that either my mama or me will have to clean these dirty children and their clothes.

"Get out of that water. Don't you see all the clothes for tomorrow wet on the line? I am not a slave, and my mama doesn't want to clean up after y'all, all day. Y'all gonna track mud up all in the house." I grab them and spank them all on the behind.

I open the door. T-Red is standing in the doorway. "Don't you ever put your fucking hands on my children again."

Kojo and Meemee begin to laugh at and point their tongues. T-Red grabs them and walks back in the house. I stand there, not able to move.

Tiny whispers, "He's so damn mean. I hate him. I wish I could leave this damn place and never come back. I hate that evil son-of-a-bitch. He is always starting shit in this house. We can never be happy as long as he's here."

I go into the house. T-Red is watching television like nothing happened. Kojo and Meemee are both on his lap. They are telling him how their day went. Meemee points her tongue at me, and Kojo can't stop laughing.

Maymay is in the kitchen cleaning up and mopping the floor. Mama is making pecan candy and Kool-Aid. The meat sauce that Maymay started isn't fully cooked. Maymay has a chicken out to fry. Everybody wants me to fry the chicken on stamp day.

I season the chicken and fix up the spaghetti by cooking it more and making more sauce.

"I'll take the clothes to Mrs. Canoe's house and dry them in her automatic dryer. You don't have to worry about nothing, Mama. I'll take care of that for you. I'll only dry the children's clothes, since they have to go to school tomorrow. I'll hang the rest of the clothes in the morning before I leave for school. I can do it. You know how I always need to stay busy. I'll help you." I tell my mother.

"I'll hang the clothes," yells Maymay from the bathroom as she cleans the muddy tub with Comet. "I don't want the Black Fuckers looking at you in your nightgown in the morning,"

I serve the kids, Maymay, and T-Red the spaghetti and fried chicken. I head for Mrs. Canoe's house with the laundry basket full of clothes.

I help Mrs. Canoe every day after school. For a moment, I can leave the chaos at home and have my own place to relax and settle down.

Mrs. Canoe has five chores for me every day. My first chore is to say "Good afternoon, ma'am." Second, she has me empty her toilet bucket. She has a toilet in her house, but it's hard for her to walk to the bathroom all the time, so she keeps a toilet bucket. Then, I sweep and mop the kitchen with Pine Sol. Then, I make the beds and dust. My last job is to read the big letter *Bible* with all the beautiful pictures and the special red words to her.

After today, I want to read about David, a powerful man who overcomes his enemies. My mama and Maymay have enemies we can't see. I have people who call me trash, throw things at me, and try to beat me every day. My life is hard.

They pull my hair so much, I wonder why I'm not bald headed yet. Maymay always tells me, "Don't let those little, black, nappy-headed girls pull yo' hair. It's going to fall. You knock the shit out of them. I don't mind coming to school if you defending yourself." T-Red showed me how to punch, and what he calls "clip" people.

The rain is gone now, and the sun is shining. I make my way over to Mrs. Canoe's house, which is about a half a mile away from Maymay's house.

"Hello, ma'am, how are you doing today? Good afternoon"

"Hey, come on in, Celeste. You know what you have to do. Where you going with all them clothes?" Mrs. Canoe asks from the blue La-Z-Boy chair in the living room. I didn't want her to see that I had a basket full of clothes. I was going to try to sneak the clothes pass her, but I didn't know that someone had moved her chair closer to the door.

"I didn't want to go to Smitty's washeteria, because I am saving money for an emergency, like if one of my sisters needed school supplies or a treat for school. My mother rarely thinks about me. I don't want to call her selfish, but I think she is more of a child." I say. "My mother left all the clothes on the line, and now I just need to dry a few of these clothes so that we will have something clean to wear tomorrow. We don't have too many decent outfits to wear. Remember how I told you that they call us trash on the bus?"

"I'll let you do it this time, girl, but don't try to sneak nothing past me. Remember what the *Bible* says."

"Thou shalt not steal," I say.

Mrs. Canoe's wrinkled forehead is now relaxed, and she looks at me, concerned. "I don't care what those little uncivilized children say. You is good people. You look out for everyone on this lonesome street—especially old people, like me." Mrs. Canoe grabs one of my long braids. "Celeste, look at me in the eye."

She holds my face and says, "You is good people. Just because your mama have all of them illegitimate children and don't know the names of them mens who messed with her don't mean all of y'all is trash." She does not let me turn away. She makes me look into her old, kind eyes.

"Let me tell you something, Celeste, because I'm not going to be with you always. You will remember the words of this old lady who helped you on this rainy day. One day, you mark my words, you gonna be somebody. You make good grades. You read the *Bible* like a schoolteacher, and you good at saving money and doing your business. Look at me!" Mrs. Canoe says.

I don't like looking at people in their eyes. I look at the clean white linoleum floor. "Mrs. Canoe, I need to get back to work before it gets dark. My grandmother says there are men in the sugar cane that will hurt me. She will make me get a switch from her tree, if I come back with the street light on," I say as I drag the basket from the porch.

"I see you putting those clothes in the dryer, girl. Let me tell you. I didn't always have a dryer. You know what you can do next time you are in a fix?" Mrs. Canoe says as she grabs the *Bible* from her chair.

"What can I do?" I ask.

"You can take those clothes one by one and hang them around your house," Mrs. Canoe says matter-of-factly.

"I didn't think of that." I look thoughtfully at the heap of wet clothes next to the Whirlpool dryer. Doing that would have been better than trying to lie to Mrs. Canoe.

I get a dollar a day for completing all five chores from Monday to Friday. On Friday, Mrs. Canoe gives me twenty-five dollars.

On Saturdays, I cook. Mrs. Canoe always wants a grand Sunday dinner like a yard chicken, pork chops, steak, or turkey wings with greens, rice dressing, jambalaya, corn bread dressing, or okra. I don't tell anybody that I secretly save money by selling food from Maymay's garden to people around Belle Place. Mrs. Canoe is one of my few customers.

We go to church together in the Mount Mariah's church van. She is in the missionary society. On missionary and communion Sunday, Mrs. Canoe wears her white polyester dress and her white hat with white shoes.

"Where do you want to read from today, Mrs. Canoe?" I ask.

"Why don't you pick one? I like it when you pick," Mrs. Canoe says.

"You know I love the words in red. I want to read the beatitudes," I say.

I read: "Blessed are the merciful for they shall obtain mercy."

"Can I give a testimony like they do in church?" I say.

"Go ahead," Mrs. Canoe says.

"You showed me so much kindness today and every day. I want you to know that you are my safe place. You are my wilderness in this dry land. If it hadn't been for your grace that God has bestowed upon you, I would be trash like my mother and family. I will forever love you;" I say and hug Mrs. Canoe."

Mrs. Canoe smells like rose perfume. Her breath smells like the peppermints she sucks when her sugar is low.

"Let's pray," Mrs. Canoe says.

"Our father which art in heaven
Hallowed be thy name
Thy kingdom come
Thy will be done
On earth as it is in heaven
Give us this day
Our daily bread
And forgive us our debts as
We forgive our debtors

Lead us not into temptation
But deliver us from evil
For thou art with thee
Thy rod and thy staff they comfort thee
Thou preparest a table before thee in the
Presence of thine enemies
Thou annoistest thou head with oil
Thou rod and thy staff shall follow
Thee all the days of thine life
Heavenly father I thank you for today's day
You looks over me while I slept and slumbered
My bed is not my cooling board
You woke me up early this morning clothed in my right mind
Ready to face another day.
I thank you father."

Tears begin to pour from my eyes, first slowly, and then so fast that my head begins to swell again. I am soaking Mrs. Canoe's soft, mushy bosom.

"That's the Holy Spirit, child. The Holy Spirit. I'll see you tomorrow. Remember what I said about them clothes," Mrs. Canoe says and winks.

When I get home, there is no more pecan candy or fried chicken. Someone has taken the bowl and placed it in the refrigerator as though there is some left, but I have learned that if it's not covered on the stove, I am not to eat it. I eat whatever is left of the spaghetti.

Bumblebee comes out of the restroom with her plate of food and yells, "Carry y'all asses to the car and let's get out of here." Her children follow behind her. She walks like the mother hen, and they walk like little chicks behind her.

Chapter 10

He Done Changed His Voice

Celeste

"Bumblebee is a fat, lazy, black bitch," Maymay says as she folds Bumblebee's clothes.

Bumblebee placed the clothes on Maymay's table that morning and said, "You, Celeste, and Tut don't work all day, like me. Folding these clothes will give you something to do. Y'all home all day, so y'all can do this favor for me."

"That woman is too lazy to be lazy. If T-Red wouldn't help me so much, I would tell her to fold her own clothes," Maymay says.

"This don't make no sense," Mama says as she holds out one of Bumblebee's panties. "What in the hell is this? I didn't know they made kinky drawers this size." We all laugh.

Bumblebee's silk panties are red and huge. They have little girl ruffles on the back of them. I imagine Bumblebee's butt swallowing this panty whole.

I say, "It's amazing how they have a brand new washer and dryer, and they can't dry or fold their own clothes. They are too selfish. They never let us use their washer and dryer for emergencies. You go to Bumblebee's trailer, and it is so clean. You come here and the dirt and food that their children bring is all over the floor. You mop the floor and they track up right back up. I don't try to clean when they are here. I give up. They eat all of the food Maymay buys with the food stamps here, and when you go to their house, they hide all the food."

Maymay looks at me and says, "Watch what you say in front of them children. They going to go back and tell they mama."

"I read to Mrs. Canoe every day from the *Bible*. One day I read, 'If a man doesn't work he shouldn't eat.' Well, Bumblebee would be a lot skinnier and her children would all be dead by now, because I do all of the work and none of them help me. Every time I cook something, they run to the pot. They eat and pile the plates on the table for me to clean like they at some fancy restaurant," I say.

T-Red sneaks in through the back door. He stands there and listens to us with his hands crossed across his muscular chest. He laughs and says, "Well, dat's what my kin women t'ink of me. Well, I'll be damn. Ain't that some shit?"

He spits out a huge laugh. "Oh, I'm just joking—I'm not mad at you." He slaps me on the shoulder. "You gonna babysit for me while I go to church wit' Bumblebee tonight?" T- Red is still laughing at me.

"You didn't pay me last time, and you said that I could eat anything I wanted, but when I ate Bumblebee's cookies, I had to walk in town the next day and buy her some more cookies," I say.

"You can watch TV and sit in my air conditioning—that's enough. This time, bring your own food. You know how Bumblebee is. She hides food from me under the bed," T-Red says.

"Tut, let me talk to you for a minute." T-Red pulls a small chunk of Mama's hair.

"What you want? I got to fold all of these clothes for Bumblebee, or she says she not gonna take me shopping at the garage sales this weekend," Mama whines.

I move even closer to the door so that I can hear them. There is a small opening in the door, and I peep inside.

"Smitty tells me that you been talking to another nigger in the fields," T-Red says and looks at Mama as if he is about to hit her at any minute. His forehead is wrinkled and he stands tall over Mama's skinny body.

"Dat's not true," Mama says, defending herself. She doesn't look at T-Red. She begins to play with her hair and look innocent.

"He says you brought him pecan candy, fried chicken, and red Kool-Aid. They say you were wearing a see-through dress with yo' ass cheeks out. Just 'cause that nigger not from around here and don't know about your high yeller trashy ass, don't mean he not gonna find out. Smitty says Paul sees him drop you off in the rain. Y'all was coming from the fields. You know Maymay don't want nobody in her yard, her house, nowhere around ya. I will beat the fuck out of you if anybody tells me some shit like that again," T-Red says. He walks out of the room.

I rush away, as T-Red opens the door. I begin folding clothes with Maymay, who is in the rhythm of the work like she is spotting cane in the fields. T-Red opens the door, gives Tut one more long and mean look, and walks into the living room to watch television with his children.

Tut walks out with a big smile, still playing with her hair. She has the same look as I had when I won my fight with Windy Washington. She has a look that says, "Nobody can tell me what to do." She will not let T-Red upset her or order her around. I don't know about this guy my mama is fooling around with, but my mama looks different. I believe T-Red and the men are telling the truth. Something is different about my mama.

Now that Maymay and I are done with the clothes, Mama is all alone. Picking up a silver metal plate from the table that gives a dim reflection of her pretty face, she looks into it and says, "T-Red is not my pa. He can't tell me what to do. I am going to get what I want. I'm going to wear the pretty clothes in the windows and get me a man with a house so that I don't have to sit in the cane fields. I'm going to marry Black."

She walks like the choir does from the double doors of church, twisting their bodies to the beat gospel music. She sits on purpose across from T-Red, who sits on the sofa. Wearing tight Braxton jeans and Frankie Says Go to Hollywood shirt that she found in a trash bag of second-hand clothes Bumblebee brought home from work, she gives T-Red the same cocky look and plays with her long ponytail.

T-Red turns his long neck around and shoots her an angry look. He is holding Kojo, who plays with an old sock. The family is watching *Star Search*. He stretches his long neck towards Mama and whispers so no one else can hear, but I read his lips. "I mean it, Tut. I ain't laughing. I'm going to bust yo' ass, if you hurt my mama."

Mama just sits there and watches the show.

"No one better not sing nare-o-one of my songs. I will break every one of the TVs in this here house," Tut says slowly. She looks scary, and I don't like that look.

"You break ma floor model color TV, and I'll break your ass. Play crazy if you want to—I'll show you crazy." Maymay's look is scarier. Maymay turns, smiles, and talks to the next contestant of *Star Search*. "Go head, *cher,* sing yo' song."

Suddenly, we hear loud thunder and lightning. Maymay shouts, "Cut ma TV off. It's starting to thunder and lightning." I look outside of the open window. Long lines of bright lighting shoot through the sky like firecrackers. The sound of thunder shakes the little house, and we feel it. I close the window,

"Celeste, you know what to do—cover all of the mirrors. Tiny, unplug everything. God is trying to talk to us. When y'all done, come sit back in here with us. We got to listen to him. By the way this house shaking—he got a lot to tell us. Let's listen y'all. Tut, cut off the lights." In obedience to Maymay's life-long superstitions, everyone does as they are told.

We gather in the living room to begin to listen to the voice of the omnipresent God, as Mrs. Canoe calls Him. The family sits in darkness. The curtains are closed and everyone sits and listens in silence as we always do in a storm.

Maymay says, "Just listen to that thunder and lightning. It's not like it used to be. You know that there is a God when he can change his voice and show us he is mad with all our evil ways. He done changed his voice to show us he means business."

I hold my bony arm out. I cannot see my hand in the dark night. I listen to the weird thunder that is, indeed, different. Maymay is always right. I need to look. I take a peek. The night is black, just black. It is scary and black and wide. There is lightning every now and then, but the sky is so wide and so big and so black. The rain is heavy and pounds on the windowpane.

"Something is out there," I whisper. "Something is in that black sky. My mama is going to leave me and go to this thing out there. I can feel it."

Maymay begins her Hail Mary's to the angry sounds of the lightning and thunder, which does not break the calm and ease of her musical prayer. She never raises her voice to compete with the loudness. She just rocks and prays and prays and rocks until the thunder stops in that big, black, scary sky. With the thunder and lightning gone, all we can now hear is the rocking chair in the darkness.

Chapter 11

Church Meeting

Celeste

The next day, Bumblebee and T-Red are at their trailer so that they can get ready for church. I walk over to Bumblebee's house with my own supper: cooked mustard greens with pickled meat and fried pork chops. I won't eat Bumblebee's food, even if she offers. As soon as I am at the door of the brown and white trailer, T-Red's hunting dogs begin to bark. He keeps them in a kennel in front of the house. Those dogs scare the life out of me.

Bumblebee is peeping at me through the window and opens the door. It is freezing cold. I always admire her neatness and style. She has fancy, store-bought furniture, not from garage sales or the Salvation Army like Maymay. She has light-colored carpet that the children cannot walk on. They can only walk on the tacky plastic runners. No one can mess up her house, not even little Down-Syndrome Kojo.

Bumblebee's hair is in a huge updo that is gelled and sprayed. It is her "beehive," with spiral circles caked in her hair. She smiles, showing her gold capital B tooth. All of her nails are long, even, and polished dark brown to match her lipstick.

"I'm going to take you and yo' mama shopping next week. Just watch those children. Don't let them walk on the carpet. Keep them in they room. They can watch all the cartoons and stuff they want. I fixed some crawfish stew, and Tut made tangerine Kool-Aid. She been making Kool-Aid day and night. Something wrong with her. She done slowed down a little too much.

"The children can only drink from the Mardi Gras cups. Each of them have they own cup. Don't let them get new ones. Nobody can go in my bedroom." She smiles again.

She is trying to be so sweet, but she is so fake, and I don't like her. I hate her.

"Whatever you do, and I mean this here, do not, and I mean do *not* let Tut into my house. You know I been letting you in here a long time. You always leave my house cleaner than you found it, and you don't eat my food or go in my room. If you let Tut in my house, I will beat your and her ass. Me and Red will tag team both of y'all asses. You hear me, girl?" Bumblebee yells at me. She goes from sweet to the old, familiar, big, fat evil devil she is.

"T-Red loves him some Bumblebee," Mama tells me. "She is freaky and knows how to please T-Red in bed with that big old ass." I think that T-Red loves her so much because she cooks so well, keeps a clean house, and is so religious. I remember how Mrs. Canoe always says, "A man don't like a dirty, trifling woman."

Mrs. Canoe always says that everyone has a weakness. No one is perfect. Bumblebee's weakness is food and manipulation. My weakness is anger and judging others. I have to pray to get over the hate and judgment I have for Bumblebee. Bumblebee and T-Red are in the strictest religion in the area, but I think that they are still mean, hateful, and judgmental. I never debate the *Bible* with Bumblebee, nor visit her church, because she always thinks that her way is the right way.

Mrs. Canoe always tells me, "Never talk about religion, politics, or other people's children." She says that is how you keep a job, friends, and family. I agree with this saying, especially about talking about religion, because this is a sore spot for Bumblebee. She has strong beliefs that she never changes.

Maymay and I are the only two allowed in the Catholic church, since my mama never gave the names of my sister's daddies. Father always said that he could excuse one child but no more. I go to the Catholic church and the Baptist church with Mrs. Canoe, but I consider myself Baptist since Father refuses to bless my sisters.

The church members and Bumblebee think that my family has an "ancestral curse," as her pastor has says. One night, they decided they would pray the curse away. I remember that night.

It is midnight. Bumblebee and some of her church members secretly visit Maymay's old Creole house at night to secretly pray for Maymay, Mama, and all of us. They come at night because they think that everyone will be asleep, and no one will know that they are there. They make a prayer ring around the house and begin to speak in tongues. They throw anointing oil around the house and dig up dirt from under Maymay's porch. They put it in a plastic sandwich bag so that they can get it prayed on by their sanctified preacher.

T-Red doesn't get involved in this whole thing. He knows how Maymay feels about her house. He warns Bumblebee, but she doesn't listen. When Bumblebee tells him the day before what she plans on doing, he tells her, "You are on your own."

Maymay, who is a light sleeper, quietly watches from her small bedroom window. I am not a light sleeper, but I think I woke up because even though the ladies are not loud, they sound so weird speaking in tongues, and the whole night is just eerie. It's like that sense Mom Dot and T-Man get that something isn't right. I wake up and look outside while the other children sleep.

Even though a group of women praying around her house is strange to her, Maymay is not going to stop anyone from praying even if it is late at night. When she sees them digging up her dirt with a rusty shovel and placing it in a baggie, Maymay has had enough.

Maymay storms out of her bedroom with one of T-Man's old shotguns. The door swings open, and Maymay yells from the front porch, "Bumblebee, I've known you for ten years. I love my son T-Red to death, but you ain't nothing but a hoodoo woman, and if'n y'all don't put ma dirt back under ma porch just like you found it, I will shoot every last one of y'all in ya big fat asses, T-Red or no T-Red. He know I don't play around when it comes to ma house and ma yard. This gonna stop right here and now, or else."

Bumblebee opens her *Bible*. She looks directly in Maymay's eyes and shouts, "Don't none of y'all move. Touch not my anointed and do them no harm."

With that, Maymay shoots one round in the air and begins aiming for the ladies of Church of Prayer. The ladies scatter like ants in a broken ant pile to their green church van and speed through the long gravel road back to the main blacktop road. Maymay continues to shoot the gun in the direction of the van. She leaves a dent in the van on purpose. Being a sharp shooter, she knows how to frighten people away from her property by letting them know she means business.

Bumblebee meant what she said. She stands there with her *Bible* open and refuses to move. Maymay tells her one last time, "Put ma dirt back where you done found it, Bumblebee, or I am going to pistol whip you. I'm not playing, *non*."

T-Red, drawn by the noise, takes Maymay's dirt and places it in her bony fingers. Maymay holds on to it. She is weak and exhausted; she stares at Bumblebee who stares in return. Both don't move. They stare each other down.

We can see Bumblebee's eyes as she begins to cry. Bumblebee says, "Red, you don't understand. There is a curse. There is a curse on your family. Look at Kojo and Tut. Maymay all the time saying maybe one day Kojo gon' talk. He gon' talk. He never talk. He never moves on in life, like my other children. Kojo will never, never be able to be normal, no matter what we do. No matter how many prayers I or Maymay says she gon' pray."

Maymay says, "Baby, we got to accept Kojo, no matter what. No matter what. Look at how them people killed that little retarded girl in New Iberia. They was trying to get a demon out her. You going to drive yourself crazy about that boy and put us all in jail for not accepting what God gave us. We got to accept Kojo. No matter what. No matter what. He is ma blood. I love all ma children and grandchildren.

"We have other little *bities* in our family. That don't mean we got a curse. My grandmother says God always give them to special people he know who is going to take good care of them. Like you, Bumblebee, and T-Red. T-Red don't treat him no different. He love that little *bitie*. Notice how God never give them to mean people. Notice that. Notice that! He gives them to good people, like you and Red who never mistreat him. *Jamais*! You and Red are good people.

You just got to accept it, girl," Maymay says louder to Bumblebee who is just staring, expressionless.

We all just wait for Bumblebee to answer.

"Look how I accept Tut. I know she is *petain*, but I never turn ma back on her. Other people would throw her and her children out on the streets. I never did. Accept your cross. *Mais,* the good Lord never give us more than we can bear. I help y'all with that boy all the time," Maymay says as she yawns.

By this time, the whole family is out on the porch watching everything.

It is late, and she is tired. She holds the plastic bag with her and T-Man's earth in one hand and her shotgun in the other hand. The baggie looks like it is some prized coon she's just caught. She doesn't dump the dirt underneath the porch like she told Bumblebee to do. She holds on to it like it's her pipe and all of her other everyday treasures.

She opens the screen door and looks back to where Bumblebee is standing and says, "All these years, T-Man prayed for this house. I prayed with him. We knelt together. His and my prayers is good enough. All them years. Your prayers are not better than mine, Bumblebee. Them women prayers not better than mine," Maymay says, holding the dirt.

The next day, I listen as Maymay sits with Bumblebee and T-Red under the tree. She is so tickled with laughter. She says, "I ain't never made so many old, white women run before."

T-Red giggles as he tells Bumblebee, "I told you my *mon* don't play when it comes to her house.

Maymay says, "Seriously Bumblebee, if I ever catch you playing with ma dirt again, I am going to kick you and T-Red off ma property. I can do it, too."

I know that Maymay is serious because she is no longer laughing or smiling. She is serious as, she says, a heart attack.

"And I ain't playing. This is mine, not your'n. When you and T-Red get your property, I don't care who you let pray on your property or mess wit yo' dirt. I don't even know what religion you is. Y'all got eleven or whatever people in your church, and it's in somebody house. Y'all don't even know what you believe in. Don't mess with me, Bumblebee. I mean it. I'm your kin, but I have my limits," Maymay says.

Bumblebee tells her, "You right, this is your property. My husband done told me to respect it. I have to listen to him. I am just trying to pray that these demons leave your house. You know Kojo is retarded, Tut got a sex demon, Tiny got behavior problems, and you have nerve problems."

I can tell that Bumblebee really believes that we are all cursed.

Bumblebee says, "All of that healing he does and those prayers T-Man say in a different language are from Africa and the devil, not God. Now, I believe this land is cursed. Red says he died a hard death, and all his brothers and people before him who treat die a hard death. I am trying to pray on this land. My pastor talks about an ancestral curse. They talk about it in the *Bible*. We are cursed. We are cursed! I married in this family, and Red done cursed my womb. Even though I don't dabble in treating and in the devil, I am cursed with an ancestral curse."

Bumblebee's words and that spooky night still haunt me, but her words, "We are cursed" bother me the most.

I think about that curse a lot. I hear a voice and a light tap on the window. "Celeste, it's me. Open the door. Let me in, I've got something to tell you." It is my mama.

"Mama, you know Bumblebee doesn't like anybody in her house. She would beat both of us, with T-Red helping, if I let you in," I say from the window of the trailer.

"It's an emergency. I need to use the phone. Just pass it out of the window," Mama says. Maymay doesn't have a phone, and Bumblebee doesn't want her near the trailer, so I decide to pass the phone. I know that T-Red has his spies, so I am going to have to work quickly. I quickly hand Mama the phone from the trailer window

Mama walks a couple of feet away—as far as the cord will let her go.

"Hello, may I speak to Black?" Mama says. "Look, I can't talk long. This is Theresa. Meet me in my secret place. I'll be waiting for you. I'm going to bring my flashlight, so that you can find me."

My mother is really strange. This all seems like a dream. She has on a long, red, off-the-shoulder dress. Her hair is parted in the middle. It smells like Ivory dishwashing liquid. She has a flashlight in one hand and the phone in the other. I take the phone and close the window. She walks away into the darkness. The dress hugs her curves as she wobbles in red high heels into the dark night and starlit sky.

Chapter 12

Tut's Red Dress

Tut

I begin to walk towards my secret place. Maymay is at home watching the CBS movie of the week. I told her I was going to walk into town to visit my friend, Sally Ann. I told her I am going to baby sit. She is happy because she said that I can make some money. She don't care I am wearing a red dress and high heels. I don't think she cares anymore what I do.

I use the flashlight to find my secret place. I get closer and closer to the tree, and I look for the ribbon that marks my room. I hear an owl hooting. I turn my feet in the opposite direction to stop the hooting owl. This is an old wise trick that Maymay taught me.

It's easy to find my secret place, because there is a full moon out. Maymay always told me that when there is a full moon, someone is having a baby. Well, I'm glad it's not me.

I remember all the mean things that my mama tells me about Celeste and me. She's probably the reason why Celeste makes me hate her so much. Maymay always says, "She is so pretty. She looks a lot like you. The only thing is, she is a clean jug. You a jug filled with oil and slop. You can never be clean again." Maymay likes causing confusion tween my daughter and me.

Maymay's all the time saying, "She has so much to look forward to." Maymay is the reason why I am so jealous of my own child.

Once I am at my secret place, I take my box from its hidden place, and I lay my blanket on the floor of sugar cane. I stick the flashlight in the dirt so that it stands straight up. I can now see my room. So much of the sugar cane has been cut. Soon, my own little sugar cane patch room will be cut.

I look up at the sky. The stars are plenty. I can see the Big Dipper. It looks like a big pot, and then there is the Little Dipper. It looks like a little pot. I can smell the burnt sugar cane stalks about twenty feet away from my patch.

"Black!" I scream when I see my man's car lights through the sugar cane.

Black puts his high beams on. He sees me rushing towards him. I am his angel in this sugar cane hell. He looks at me in my red dress.

"I'm glad you came," I tell Black.

I can tell by the way look at me that he like what he sees. He doesn't say anything. He only stares.

"I brought you a picture of an angel just like I promised," I say. The lights from the car stop on me like a spotlight. The sugar cane behind me must've looked like a curtain when I came out of it to meet Black.

"I came out here because I am really worried about you. Come in the car before the mosquitoes and termites eat you alive." Black opens the door.

Once I am in the car, he gets a blanket from the back seat and helps me wrap it around myself. He takes the flashlight from my hand. He makes a big fuss about me and coddles me like a baby. I like it.

"This is no place for a young girl like yourself. You shouldn't be out here. There are wild animals, owls, and all kinds of things in these sugar cane."

I take off my high heels and rub my feet.

"This sure is a nice car. What kind of car is this?"

"It's a Buick Rivera," Black says as he smiles from the driver's seat.

I touch the oiled dashboard and rub the fur seat covers.

"This sure is a nice car," I say.

"You can look just as nice as this car if you fix yourself up every day. Some days you come in the fields all made up. Other days you look a mess. Today you look nice, but you're wearing the wrong shoes. You shouldn't wear heels to walk in the fields," he says as he looks at his dirty carpet underneath my red pumps.

"I like to take old cars and fix 'em up. Everybody be wanting me to help them fix up they rides. I'm good with cars and fixing up stuff. They buy their cars broke, and I fix them. Don't take me long. I can't read too good, but I'm sure good with my hands. They used to make fun of me in school about my French. They call me Frenchy. I was never good at books. My teacher, he is Creole, like me. He tells me to go to trade school and get a trade fixing cars. I never told him I couldn't read much." Black says.

"I don't like my nickname. It's a country girl nickname. I'm going to have a new nickname one day and a cute, little house with a lot of pretty angels watching me," I say. I don't want to talk about him. I want to leave this place.

"Well, it's good you want something. Look, I know what they say about you in the streets. The fellas in the fields remind me every day when you bring us Kool-Aid. Everybody makes mistakes. People hate you around here for no real reason. I know you have four children. I have two. Their mama tells me that she doesn't want them living with me, 'cause I'm never going to do anything in life but fix cars and work in the fields," Black says.

"I want to make an honest woman out of you, Tut. I want to take you away from your secret place and give you some of those dreams you see in that book in the sugar cane. I know you simple in the head, but you can cook and clean. I smell what you be cooking in that house, and I smell the clean smell of Pine Sol coming from that house. I know about Red and how he makes a slave out of you. I want you to come with me to Sunset." Black says.

"I know I can fix my house up real good and you can leave your children here with Maymay. Celeste will take good care of them," he says.

I can't believe that this man wants me with my slop-filled self.

"I know that Father pretty much threw you out of the Catholic Church. There are good Christian churches in Sunset. You can pick one and sing in the choir or become an usher. You only need to tell God your sins. I would go with you to church. You can get a job frying your chicken at Roger's Cajun Meat Market. We can have some more children. I am tired of being lonely. What do you think?" Black asks me.

"Do you think that I can get a double wide instead of a single wide?" I ask. I've always wanted a doublewide trailer.

"I can put two single wides together," says Black.

"I'll do it! I'll do it!" I scream. I am so excited. "I'm finally going to be able to have everything I've ever wanted."

"Pack your things, Tut. I'm going to come by and pick you up after I talk to Red. I don't want him and Maymay causing problems for us in Sunset. I want Maymay to respect our house, like we respected hers," Black says.

I say, "Wait, I want to get my box," I open the door of the Buick.

"Tut, look at me," he grabs my itty bitty waist, "You don't understand. I am taking you away from this place so that we can make dreams together. You don't need to dream anymore from catalogs. I will make all your dreams happen as best as I can, but you will dream with me, not alone. Maymay and T-Man have their dreams, Bumblebee and Red got theirs. Now it's time for you to start living your life," Black says.

I remember the story that Celeste told the children and Maymay about Lot's wife. She looked back and everything turned into a pillar of salt. I'll leave it here. My eyes are wild with hope.

That night, Black removed the pretty red dress Maymay made for me. He hugged me with those big, black muscle arms. He licked my face and began to kiss me. I decided I was going to give him the best piece of ass he ever had. I've had good sex for much less. As Maymay always say, a wet pussy and an empty pocketbook don't match. Today, I got a wet pussy and a pocketbook filled with dreams from Black. I give him all that I have, my little cane room, my moon, my stars, and what's left of the whore of Belle Place.

Black drops me off in front of Maymay's house. I close the door and run home like a child ready to open her presents under the Christmas tree. When I open the door, Maymay is peeping through the window of the living room.

"What's wrong, Maymay?" I ask. She has her .45 in her lap and is still peeping out of the curtains towards the sugar cane.

"Tut, you won't believe what happened tonight." She looks at me with wide, spooked-out eyes. She's talking in a low whisper. "All through the sugar cane, a light was flashing. Then a car drove to the sugar cane fields. It is the Big Bitch and the Black Fuckers." Maymay sits glued to the sofa and continues to peep out at the sugar cane and the moonlit sky.

Chapter 13

Tut and Black

Celeste

"You can add to the value of an Impala, Chevy, or Cadillac by fixing it, waxing it, cleaning it up, and adding new, shiny parts, but you can't make this ho yo' housewife," T-Red tells Black from the opposite side of the busted screen door.

"All I'm going to say is, think hard and long about what you gonna do. That's you, but I wouldn't do it. Any day now, that girl's reputation gon' reach Sunset. Maymay got her .45 and T-Man old shotgun. I got a .22, four hunting rifles, and six hunting dogs. But, I ain't using nare-a-one to defend that slut's honor or save her from your angry fist when you find some field nigger humping her in your bed," T-Red says.

T-Red looks through the hole of the screen door at Black, eye-to-eye. His brows are wrinkled and intense. He is okay with Black's decision to shack up with Mama. Before Black takes my mamma away to Sunset, he wants Black to know who he is getting, in case he doesn't know by now. I have a feeling he knows. He wants that wild, red dress hanging up next to his bed.

This man named Black is wearing navy blue short sleeve shirt and pants. His blue, 1975 Buick Riviera shines on our dirt road. The Buick's clean silver rims shine like Maymay's neat aluminum foil over her garlic stuffed pork roast.

Out of breath, Black wipes the sweat from his dark, chocolate-colored forehead. This Black must love my mama. As much as I hear about how much of a whore she is, or as my Maymay says, a *petain,* no man has ever visited my house. And he had to dodge six dogs just to stand in front of Maymay's door. I had to shoo the sea of barking dogs away and herd them onto the back porch. I listen as best as I can as they bark at the scent of Black's cheap Woolworth's cologne. Now, he stands on my Maymay's cypress porch and asks for permission to shack up with my mama, the town's whore.

"Don't beat no nigger and risk your life with the likes of her," T-Red tells Black. He looks at him with the same look he always gives Tut, my sisters, and me—like we are slop mud on the bottom of his shoe. "They done told you about that trifling gal. All you see is bright skin, long good hair, a fine ass, and big tiddies. Fuck Tut! You and Tut can both go to hell or Sunset, for all I care," T-Red says.

"That ho done all kind of shit to this family. She lie, she steal, and she mess with them women in town mens. She put Maymay in Pineville Mental Hospital and almost gave her a stroke, because Maymay be always having to run after them no good ass children of *hine*. The women in Belle Place would be happy to get rid of that freak." As T-Red talks about my mama, he turns his head left, rolls his eyes, and sucks his teeth at her. He then gives her the same look he's giving Black, but it's longer and harder and more hateful then it's ever been before.

"Look at ma back teef," T-Red says. He smiles what Maymay calls a Sambo smile. "They all been knocked out fighting behind Tut and all of her whoreishness." T-Red now stares at Black again, calmer now. As Maymay says, he has gotten it off of his chest.

Inside, Maymay sits in a black, leather rocking chair. Rocking back and forth and admiring her unlit pipe in her long skinny fingers, she refuses to look at Black. I am very surprised. She just rocks on that worn linoleum, which has holes in the green diamond design showing cypress wood that I am surprised has never cracked by now, like the wood on the tree swing.

I feel bad that I could not cover the huge white hole that she is sitting on. The stuffing is coming out of the chair. I've swept some of the stuffing away each morning along with dirt from the fields.

She must have rocked in that chair a million and one times, talking to herself, praying the rosary, and "calming her nerves." The rocking chair hums slowly and ticks just like the coo-coo clock.

Now, I realize why Maymay never looks at Black. She is not going to let a field hand never introduced to her come in her peaceful house and think that he deserves her attention. Maymay is just weird that way. I think about that dirt in the sandwich bag when the ladies from the sanctified church visited us.

I think of her saying, "No, no matter what they say in the streets, this is ma house; and dat's why me *et* T-man had a good life in our nice peaceful place back ya. I don't let no *petains* or field hands in ma house."

She just rocks and looks at the floor and listens. I don't think that she cares about introductions.

The two men face each other, man to man. Black stands on the porch. He is shorter than T-Red, but he has bigger muscles, dark chocolate, skin, dark brown eyes, and a bright white smile. T-Red stands inside and holds the door shut by holding it through one of the holes in the screen.

The living room smells like 10 o'clock dinner, baked chicken stuffed with garlic, smothered okra with shrimp and sausage, and pig's feet. My Maymay always tells me that she cooks early and a lot, because when she was young, people would do their hardest work in the morning with little time to cook at noon.

T-Red wipes the beads of sweat from his forehead with a red headscarf from his pocket. He places it back in his pocket and looks at Black. They look like my cousin Liver's gamecocks—ready to fight. A pregnant cat squeezes its huge kitten-filled belly through the bottom of the screen door, leaving muddy footprints on the living room floor.

Unlike T-Red, Maymay seems entertained and finally lifts her pale, wrinkled face for the first time to look at the two men. She rocks in laughter.

Her laughter is young and full. "So, you say you want to make an honest woman out of her. I'll be damn!" She strikes a match to light her pipe. "Say you're going to give her all the things she needs. *Je serai un fils de chienne.*" She darts a look at my mama. My mama doesn't look at Maymay. She just holds our hard, blue suitcase. Mama looks at Black like he is the only person in the room, and I and everyone else can feel a little of what they feel just by looking at them. She is on edge of her seat and ready to go, like Maymay always says. Before Black came, I put Bumblebee's Avon lipstick samples on Mama's lips. She wanted me to make her look pretty. It doesn't take much to make my mama look pretty.

I braided her hair into two French braids and tied two red ribbons on the bottom. Everyone was mad at me for making her look like a schoolgirl and just as young as me. My mom sat on the floor as I combed her hair. I sat on the bed. I felt like she was my child. I told them, "I have to French braid and grease her hair with coconut oil, because she won't have me there to comb her hair in Sunset. Her hair will be *py-yay* in a week or two. At least this will hold her decent for a while." They all agreed and were so proud of me for thinking ahead.

Tut wears the Diana Ross red dress again. It is special. It is her feel-good dress, similar to one she sees in the window of her favorite store, Sunflowers, in town.

Maymay has sewn the dress with no pattern—only a stern look at the dress from outside of the store. The dress compliments Mama's soft, flawless, olive skin and her light green eyes. She still wears the chipped red finger nail polish from two days ago. She wears red jellybean sandals and chipped red matching toenail polish.

Looking at Mama this Friday afternoon on company day, you would swear everyone is talking about someone else. Who is the slut, *petain*, or home wrecker T-Red shouts about in Maymay's living room? Mama looks innocent, young, harmless, and fragile. How can this beautiful woman with the cutest dimples and red ribbons tied at the bottom of her hair like a nice little Catholic schoolgirl have the worst reputation in Belle Place?

Maymay continues talking with her company from the rocking chair, "Hold on while I smoke my pipe some mo'. I don't smoke it often, *petit garcon*. Only smoke it when there's something good and juicy to talk about. All these years, I can't join the talk. Thanks to Tut, talk has always been about me and my family. Yeah," she pauses for a moment and stares as if in deep thought. "Yeah," she says shaking the ponytail and looking at mama, "Thanks to you, Tut."

"They never remember all the favors T-Man did for them. Treating people here with headaches, backaches, earaches, and all kinds of aches. He would take care of other people before he take care of his own family problems and wouldn't take a nickel for it. The doctor would always tell people, 'Go to T-Man. If you got the faith, go to T-Man. He can do things, when I can't.'"

Maymay looks at T-man's picture. There is so much hurt in her eyes, as she tries to resist the tears in front of the company. She lost the strong Maymay in her voice and her eyelashes flutter quickly. Everyone knows that she is fighting her tears.

"He would treat them with his hands and shake out the sickness here on my property like he is shaking dirt from his hands. Only he is shaking demons, Cushma, and all, on *our* property. Bumblebee had to tell me that them people left they demons here for us to fight off and for us to have the misery.

"She tells me that all of that stuff comes from Africa where they worship the devil. I don't believe everything that crazy gal say. *Mais*, I believe that though after seeing how ma family done change now. Bastille used to be a good name along the Bayou Teche and especially in Belle Place. People used to smile at that name. People used to swear to they children on that name. Now that name not worth a pot to pee in nor the window to throw it out."

Taking a long smoke from the pipe, she kicks the black and white pregnant mama cat. She yells, "*Chat, Chat!* Get that cat out of here before she has them babies in my clothes or eat out ma pot on the table."

One of the children runs through the kitchen, catches the cat, and throws it outside.

Maymay continues her speech. "Bumblebee and T-Red say that's why Tut hot and Kojo a little retarded *bitie*. Them people left all they demons here on MY property. Now they say we hoodoo people. Now they say we crazy people. Now they say we is trashy people. Helping people out, though!"

Maymay's sadness turns into much anger. She gives the rocking chair one strong pound and grip as she stops it. "After T-Man started treating people, Cushma start riding me and the girls more, and Tut start getting pregnant," Maymay takes another long, intense smoke from her pipe. She looks into the green and white linoleum. She pauses in a moment of deep thought. She blows a huge cloud of smoke in Black's direction. The smell of tobacco is so much stronger than it usually is when Maymay smokes her pipe.

"Hurry up and get off ma property. The only reason you standing by ma door is 'cause T-Red tells me you want to make an honest woman out of Tut. You said it to the field hands. Any man who is saying something good about Tut around Belle Place deserves my high time," she says.

Maymay looks at her television and the clock to her left. She points to the television with her black pipe. "At this time, I could be watching *One Life to Live*, and the rest of my stories, or I could be stirring ma pot over yonder on the stove. So don't start talking stupid, *non.*" Maymay crosses her skinny legs and bows her head into the pipe so that she can get another smoke.

She makes little O's with the smoke, which all of us love to watch. The children sit watching the dancing family of mama and papa O's.

"Tobacco's too high. I'm only going to smoke this on good occasions," Maymay laughs with smoke escaping her mouth.

Maymay then begins a loud conversation with Mama, as if no one else is listening. "Well, Tut now you're going to have your pretty clothes you see in the window in town and your doublewide trailer. After all of these years, you are going to have the things in all of them magazines you carry all the time. Ummm Humm." She winks at Mama and bites into the pipe. "I'm really happy for you, Girrrl." She nods and winks at Mama. "*Mais,* that's good." Leaning her head back and rolling her eyes and pressing her lips tightly together, she begins to stare at the ceiling as she pauses and thinks for a while.

Bending forward and turning to Mama again, she continues in her loud full-volume speech, "It's a miracle that this young handsome Black man wants to shack up with you. I always tell y'all try to find people your own color, but you all go out and marry these *chocalat femme et homme,*" Maymay smiles and laughs at her own joke. "Y'all bring nappy-headed little children with all them cuklebugs. I'm the only one of the Bastille sisters left with black, nappy-headed grandbabies," Maymay yells in amusement as she looks at the children sitting on the floor around her chair. Normally she would tell them, "Y'all go outside and play. This is grown folk's business." On this day, I think Maymay wants to teach all of us with Mama being the subject of her lesson. She forgets that she and T-Red are using bad language in front of the well-behaved, attentive little ones.

"He is willing to forgive all of your many sins. *Mais*, that's a miracle." Maymay now turns her attention to T-Red who is stuck to Maymay's words like green flies on her fly swatter. "T-Red you ought not tell that gal we not gon' be yonder for her. She still your family, *petain* and all; her name is Tut Bastille. The Bastille family will always be there for one another. No matter what! We don't turn our back on our family, *non. Jamais*! Let me explain what's going to happen if she messes up for her a little mo'."

Maymay stops the rocking and holds the pipe away from her lean body. Leaning forward in the chair, she says slowly and clearly in her best English-speaking voice as she now looks in Mama's eyes, "If you mess this one up, I'm going to walk…Wait a minute let me put this high tobacco down to let you know I mean business." She places the pipe on the table next to her chair. Grabbing Mama's tiny body by the shoulders and shaking her as if she is a rag doll, she gives Mama a long intense look.

Maymay says, "I'm going to walk to Sunset in all of this hot sun and shoot you with the .45 me and T-Man keep in the filing cabinet if you mess up your one last chance of happiness for something stupid."

Mama smiles at Maymay as she does this, but Maymay is very serious and does not smile. "Don't you crack a smile, Tut. I'm serious," Maymay says.

Maymay thinks that shacking up is good for Mama because she is a whore, and at least now she will have someone providing for her. She won't have to have sex anymore for favors. Maymay always tells her, "*Un sac vide et un seche chatte ne correspondent pas.*" I ask Bumblebee what that means, and she tells me that it means a wet pussy and an empty purse doesn't go together. She says I am old enough to know what it means.

"*Mais*, yeah, I told you your whole life is over after you had all of them children. No one would want you with four children. Not even the Black Fuckers who hide in the sugar cane want you 'cause you dried up from men using you anyway that they know how. Well, this is really your last chance."

"Are any of the children going?" I ask. I know that I will never leave, because I need to help Maymay and Bumblebee. I also know that I am too old to hang around a young man like Black.

Maymay looks at Black as though she already knows the answer. She stares at Black as though they are the only two in the room. Her eyes are filled with humor, and she looks like she knows what he is going to say before he says it. There is a long pause as everyone waits for the answer that my Maymay knows as she shakes her head up and down and rocks steadily, calmly, and softly. The pipe is fixed at the corner of her mouth, and she inhales the tobacco that is now gone. The children get up and turn around to face Black and continue their seating arrangement in the opposite direction.

"Well, nigger, speak up," T-Red yells. He is furious, and his voice is loud and threatening as he pushes forward to wait for the last bit of conversation.

"I don't have enough room for the three children. I only have a two-bedroom, single-wide trailer." Black looks at the hole in the screen door and runs his hands through it. "Y'all can come by and visit every now and then," he whispers.

Maymay slowly moves her head to look at Mama. She stares at her instead of Black, even though she's talking to Black. "Mister, let me tell you something. I wouldn't expect you or Tut to raise ma grandchildren, ma dogs, ma cats, and even ma hogs. Tut can barely even raise herself with her simple mind. Some days, she cleans my whole house, spotless. Other days, she leaves it all *disorde* for me and Celeste to clean. She got the worse reputation in Louisiana. I can't bear a week, let alone a month in some bed in Pineville or the hospital again. I like to kill her before with a butcher knife after the last bastard child. If she gone, maybe me and ma family can one day lift our heads in public before I die and pass away like poor T-Man." Maymay is serious about this, and she makes the sign of the cross when she mentions my granddaddy.

Maymay turns, smiles at Mama, and picks up her usual speed. "You happy now, huh *cher*? Girl, you hell. That man gon' take you'n after you had four children and a bad reputation—worse one. Thought I'd never see the day. *Mais*, I would be happy, too. Wait a minute!" Maymay stops rocking as she spots the suitcase in Mama's hand.

She gets up and grabs the suitcase. "Give me that damn suitcase. That's our only suitcase in the house. Suitcase too high! We only use them for good occasions in case we have to be around people and conduct decent business. It's not for you to use. I leave you take ma suitcase and I never see it again. Leave ma shit here. Use them pillowcases off of the line outside," Maymay stands with the precious suitcase in her hand. It is used for hospital visits, field trips, and overnight stays. It is important to us.

T-Red explodes like a firecracker. Grabbing Mama's suitcase from Maymay's old, delicate fingers in a fit of rage, he begins to empty it. "Get the hell out of my mama's house." He kicks everything that is on the floor outside in the grass with the chickens and dogs. "Take this country gerry girl nigger wit' you. You sorry bitch. How in the fuck you gon' deny your own children, your flesh and blood, for some country Frenchy John in the fields you just met?" He begins collecting the clothes from the porch in handfuls. He dumps them into the front yard. The children run outside to watch the show.

"Don't come back. When I get my mama a phone, I'm going to block your number. None of them girls are going to go to your house. Next t'ing you know you'll be letting that nigger mess with your own flesh and blood just so you can have some double wide trailer, and outdo me and Bumblebee." It feels like an earthquake in Louisiana.

"Leave, leave, and don't come back. Maymay is dead right. Me and ma children will finally be able to lift our eyes and look people in the face. Get out. Never come back. I mean that." He stands like a giant on the little porch and throws my mama's last thing from the suitcase, my cigar box filled with loose change. It hits my mama on the corner of her forehead. She is too happy to cry or complain. She gets up and runs to the shiny car. Covering her mouth with the red chipped nail-polished covered fingers, she tries to hide her huge smile.

Although there is a lot of commotion, Maymay is dosing off as she calls it, and she is mumbling something under her breath and picking up speed on her rocking chair like a farmer tilling his garden on a hot day, picking up the fertile soil and shooting it in air.

The sound of the rocking chair floats through the quiet space of the room. The sound is so familiar on this strange day. As long as Maymay and T-Man live in that house with all of us, we know it very well. It is like the beating of our own hearts.

Maymay holds on to her rosary. Everyone can tell that she is saying her Hail Mary's for Mama's safety and happiness. She does love my mama, even though it seems like she hates her. She wants her to be happy. I feel like I've lost a friend.

Maymay smiles peacefully and rests, knowing that Mama can start a new life. She wants to see her daughter's dreams come true just as she wanted Mama to have that red Diana Ross dress from Sunflowers. "You're prettier than that woman," I remember she told Mama, as she knelt at the bottom of the dress to fix the hem.

"If only you would have made the right choices in life, you could have had any man you wanted, Tut—any man," Maymay told Mama as she looked up at her in that day she sewed my mama that dress.

The children scatter outside to play their childhood game of Mother May I? Now that the special occasion of the pipe and company are over, they have found some new fun. No one dares to question Maymay's decision. Maymay always knows best.

One of the children shouts, "Mother may I take four tiny steps?"

The leader yells, "Yes, you may!"

The sky is so blue today. It is so beautiful. There are no white clouds, only blue. The sky is pretty like my mama. I am happy for her.

I bet she thought for sure that T-Red was going to mess up her dream of moving in with Black. I put the clothes in the trunk of the car.

I tell Black, "He who finds a wife finds a good thing." I hold my mama's hand.

The clean and handsome Black whispers at the clothes and white pillowcases covered with chicken poop. "I don't plan on marrying your mother," he says. "We are just going to shack up."

He slams the trunk. "I got two children from my lawfully married wife. That's why I can't take y'all. I'm paying child support now. I can't afford no more children," Black says.

Mama says, "I have always been proud of you. Everybody knows you are going to make something of yourself. You speak good and you are smart. You are beautiful. You look prettier than me. You will have everything I always wanted. I haven't told you this before, but sometimes I've been jealous of you, not because I hate you but because you are so perfect. One day, you are going to take those braids out of your hair and let your hair run wild like me for someone you really want," Mama says.

"If I stay here one more day doing stuff for Bumblebee and T-Red, Maymay, and all of y'all, I'll end up in a bed at Pineville like Maymay once did, but nobody gonna come for me," Mama says. I know she is telling me the truth.

"I won't be good to y'all, either way. I want you to go to the tree that I told you about whenever we walking. There is a red ribbon tied in the sugar cane. That's my secret place. Go there when you miss me. I have a box there with all of my catalogs and some more of my favorite things. You and the girls will have fun out there like me and my brothers did when we were young." My mama gives me a strong, rare hug.

"I will go there. I promise," I say. "You don't have to worry about any of us, Mama. I will take care of the children. You can have the twenty dollars in change that I earned. I can earn more. Don't worry about any of us. Please, I just want you to know one thing. I am not perfect. I have bad thoughts. I want harm to come to my enemies, and sometimes I look at dirty pictures in magazines and masturbate. I am growing every day, and people don't want me to be like you. Bumblebee says my womb is surely cursed. It's hard doing better in life when people expect you to do badly. All I can do is try," I say.

My mother is surprised about my honesty. I'm not surprised by hers. I don't cry. Neither does she, even though Maymay always tells me that crying cleanses your soul. I push my pain somewhere deep inside of me. T-Man once told me he knew a man who never knew pain. He would cut cane and work so hard that, even if he cut himself, he would still work while the blood would drain from his body. I think my mama and me are like that. Something is wrong with our heads. We don't feel pain.

She doesn't tell the rest of the children good bye. They are not concerned about her, anyway. In my mama's same happy spirit, they play Mother May I? Mama runs childlike to the passenger seat of the Buick Rivera and wraps her long arms around Black. All I can hear is Al Green's "Living for the Love of You" fading in the blue sky and all I can see is that red dress dragging from the bottom of that Buick in the dust clouds of the dirt road. Soon they are gone, and the house is filled once more with the sound from the rocking chair in tune with our hearts.

Chapter 14

Continuity

Celeste

I find the red ribbon which led to my mama's little *Gilligan's Island* house with no roof. The floor is mashed like someone has stepped on the sugar cane. I find a rusty metal box hidden in the ground.

I use my mama's art supplies and write, "There is a sense of continuity in spirit, love, and laughter as long as your children carry your dreams after your life." I feel like my mama is sitting next to me, all pretty and soft, as we look through the catalogs. I miss her songs and her big kisses. She was like a little sister to me.

Soon they'll cut the cane, but I'll have mama's box and memories. There is the Big Chief tablet that my mother used to write songs by Diana Ross in.

One of my favorite words is "continuity." When I think of that word, I think about T-Man, the healer who passes his healing to my mother. I think about my sisters. I think about being fourteen now and having my own children one day and sharing what I've learned. Continuity is Belle Place. Things happen the same way every time, like the bookmobile that gets me over my summer boredom.

One day, I tell Ms. Canoe, "There are no good shows on TV. That's the only thing that I have to do: watch TV."

Mrs. Canoe tells me, "Pray for something good, then." We did, and a week later the bookmobile comes, and it is the highlight of my summer.

It is on time at 10 a.m., a white mobile home that parks on the narrow gravel shoulder. There, I can find all kinds of books to read.

The librarian is Ms. January, a sixty-year-old white lady who wears her glasses on the tip of her nose, and she always introduces me to the books that will help me in college and school.

As I sit on the floor in the *Gilligan's Island* hut with no roof, I read prayer cards that Mama received in catechism. She has about fifty prayer cards and rosaries. Now, I believe that she did steal from the church, as Father accused her.

I find a prayer card with a picture of the Virgin Mary. She is dressed in my sister's and my favorite color, Virgin Mary sky blue. Mrs. January once told me that she wears this pretty blue color because it represents the color of the sky. It is called "pure sky."

I think of continuity and Maymay in her rocking chair saying the prayers over and over. I look at the pretty blue gown that the Virgin wears. I think about how awesomely blue the sky was when my mother said goodbye. I read the prayer on the card:

Holy Mary, Mother of God, pray for us sinners, now and at the hour of our death. Amen.

I think that Mary is looking down at me from the pure sky and praying for me. I think about Maymay. What sins has she committed? She is always talking about my Mama's sins, but I think that somewhere in the past, Maymay had sins of her own. I wonder if when she undressed, did she touch her own curves? Did she admire her own body? Did she touch herself and think about T-Man? I think of my Maymay and her perfect matching slips. She is such a perfect lady.

I think about Mrs. Canoe, who is now in the Old Folk's home in town when I read at the hour of our death. Maymay says that she will die soon because she is really sick. She only has hours, not days, to live. I want to see her, but I don't have a ride.

This is my first and last visit to my mama's secret place. I'll ask T-Red for a ride. I never ask him for anything.

I walk in the front door and ask T-Red, "Will you take me to see Mrs. Canoe?"

He is in T-Man's La-Z-Boy in Maymay's living room. His children are sitting on his lap. "There is a train that goes into town. You can hop a train," he says. He doesn't look back. He is watching *The Flintstones* with his children.

Listening to the conversation from the kitchen while she is canning figs the children picked from trees, Maymay yells, "That's too dangerous. She can scratch her face or her big, fine, pretty, red legs trying to hop the train. One of the strange men can rape her, and she will end up all used up, like her no good mo'." She spoons freshly cooked figs in sanitized jars.

T-Red says, "As always, Maymay is right. It wouldn't look right. You are such a pretty girl. You are more like Maymay and Bumblebee every day. I forget you're fourteen. You still wear them plaits in your head. You always trying to look like a tomboy, but these men still find your womanhood. They have bad people here, Celeste." T-Red stops talking for a while and focuses on the television. He and the children are now laughing. I listen intently for his next words and decisions.

"You can hop it with my son Liver. Liver hops trains all the time. He cuts grass in town for a lot of white people. Sometimes he even carries my old lawn mower with him. Hop it with him," T-Red says. There is a commercial now, so T-Red for the first time turns around to talk to me.

"I know that I was mean to your mama, Celeste, but you have really come through for all of us. You'll probably be the first person to go to college in this family. Do you see how everything is nice and quiet here now that your mama is gone? Well, that's how we need to keep it. Liver will take care of you. Hop a train with him," T-Red says.

Chapter 15

Let Your Hair Hang Loose!

Celeste

I wake up to the rooster crowing. It stands on the propane tank outside my window. It looks one-eyed at me through the dirty screen and window. I run to the bathroom and pour my bath water. My sister, Tiny, peed on me. Maymay doesn't seem to bother everybody as much as she used to about the water, and now I have a deep bath with bubbles. My body aches from cleaning the yard the day before.

My breasts are full, and I admire them. My body is muscular and firm from so much work. I touch myself. This has been a secret of mine for some time. Mrs. Canoe told me that this is a sin and it increases the fire inside of young women like me. I am now fourteen about to be fifteen, and it seems like my body is changing with each passing day.

This releases a lot of stress for me. I think about how everyone thinks that I am perfect. I cry as I feel the ecstasy, because I know that I am not perfect like they think I am. If T-Red knew how I wasn't so perfect, would he hate me like my mama? If he knew that I felt my own pussy, would he kick me in the chicken coup?

Maymay is at the bathroom door when I open it.

"I don't want you using all of that water to take a bath. I haven't been telling you anything, but I'm still listening, Celeste," Maymay says. She looks at me like she knows my secret.

"Why you wearing plaits? You need to get Bumblebee to put you one of them perms she got. You're always pressing everybody else hair. You need to take care of your own hair. Your hair is neat, but you need to grow up and wear your hair nice like people your age.

You need to wear nice clothes. I'll sew you stuff, Celeste. I'll sew you whatever you want me to sew," Maymay says. She touches the braids that I wear in my hair.

"Your hair is so pretty. I want to see your hair in a perm," she continues to plead with me.

I go to the kitchen, and I fix me a bowl of oatmeal and some coffee. I don't worry about my hair. It's not a big deal. I don't want to bring attention to myself. Maymay looks sad now and concerned. I don't even know why she's so worried about me. Hair and clothes are not important to me. She sits next to me.

"Celeste, this is the time young women figure out where they are going to go in life. Your mother had you when she was your age. She knew who she was. She liked men, boys, and old men. She was hotter than ma cast iron pan when it has got grease in it. She was special. Me and T-Man could never forgive ourselves when she had you," Maymay says. She stops and stares at me for a few seconds.

"We watched her, but not enough. T-Man couldn't carry the shotgun with him and get the man what did it, 'cause she never told nobody. She never told nobody about who done it. Then I let ma guard down, and she keeps ho-ing around. People can blame us all they want. They don't know that Tut is special and you can't treat her like everybody else. I almost think that none of it was her fault. It's all spiritual, like Bumblebee say."

I don't say a word. I just sip my coffee. I know that the best thing for Maymay is to listen. I just listen. Maymay likes when you listen.

"Bumblebee works for this rich, white doctor in town. She says she got some clothes they done give her. They got a rich granddaughter. She's picky. She got clothes that got the tags on them. Some of them still got the dry clean bags on them. Shoes are still in the box. I want you to go through them, Celeste. You're going yonder to that thing at school. I want you to put your best foot forward. I want you to make us all look good. I don't want you in them plaits. I rarely tell you what to do. You always listen. You never talk back, but I want you to promise you will do this for me. I want you to promise that you will go there and make the Bastilles look good," Maymay says, and she goes to the closet in her room and takes out a lawn-sized trash bag with clothes.

She empties the contents on the table and orders me to pick out what I want. It's just as she says. Some of the clothes still have the tags on them and some are in dry clean bags. Bumblebee didn't think much of me. She could have left the clothes hanging. All this will do is bring attention to me. I do something I rarely do. I begin to say no.

I say, "Maymay, perms cost too high. I don't want to do my hair because I'll have to keep doing it, and Tut told me that my hair is going to turn nappy with a perm. I can get Bumblebee to put braids in my hair. I can buy beads," I say.

I am now done with my coffee and oatmeal, and I just stare at the clothes that have expensive price tags. "As for the clothes, I have a weird shape. T-Red says that I am shaped like a boy. I won't look right. I like wearing my same clothes. I'm just a little funny that way. I don't want to draw attention to myself. Besides, I've been reading the autobiography of Malcolm X, Nikki Giovanni, James Baldwin, Maya Angelou, and a lot of other people who say that we've got to love ourselves—that includes our hair and everything." I am talking to Maymay, but she doesn't hear me. She is going through the piles of clothes. This has been the first time that I have ever spoken up for myself to Maymay.

"I don't know who all of those people are. I don't care who they are. I just know that you need to look pretty and make us look good. People don't wear braids anymore. This is the eighties. Afros and braids were in the seventies. I remember, because Tut wanted braids and her hair was too soft," Maymay says. She throws a yellow suit at me. "Go try this on."

"Maymay, I am going to read 'Ego Tripping' by Nikki Giovanni. Ms. January gave me a dashiki. We have everything planned. I walk to the public library every Monday after school, and we practice." I say, "She went through a lot of trouble to get that dashiki for me. She has a daughter who is married to a Nigerian, and he had it shipped from Africa. She paid for it, and she is going to display it in the library for Black History Month, which they don't celebrate at our school. I always tell her to be careful, because people around here don't like changes, but she has been introducing us to books that people don't like. She is a sweet lady." I fold the wrinkled yellow suit with the price tag on it and hand it back to Maymay. I go to the closet and pull out the dashiki.

"She even told me how to wear it and how to take care of it," I say.

"What are you trying to do, Celeste? Are you trying to do like your mama and make us shame again? T-Red is even excited about your trip. He is going to bring you to school all the way in Lafayette and everything. You can't go there dressed like an African. For sure people will think that we dabbling in hoodoo and stuff. You give that back to that lady, or I am going to whip you. I haven't whipped you in a long time, but I will whip you, Celeste. I will," Maymay says. She looks into my eyes, and I know that she is serious.

"Now, take this suit and go in that restroom. After you are done trying the suit on, I will alter it so that it fits perfectly on you and your bad shape, as you say. I will make it fit right on you. After I alter that dress, I want you to take those four plaits out of your pretty long hair, and I want you to wash and condition it with that good shampoo. When it dries, I will press your hair and curl it, and you will go to that competition and make us all proud on Saturday. From that day on, you are going to wear what I tell you to wear. Until you can do for yourself, you will do what I tell you to do, or you will go to live with your mama," Maymay says, and I know that she is serious.

That day, the yellow dress finds and reveals the beautiful curves of my body. According to Maymay, I am shaped very different. All the years she has sewed for others, she has never altered an outfit for such a perfect shape. That's what Maymay told me. Maymay even finds matching yellow pumps for me, even though I've never worn heels.

Maymay presses my hair and curls it. Bumblebee and the girls look on as Maymay does my hair and alters my suit. They tell me how beautiful and different I look. The children tell me I look like a woman and not a child. Maymay always tells me that young children say the truth, so I believe them.

"I didn't know that Tut, I mean, Celeste, had tits and ass," T-Red says as he watches Maymay make the final alterations on the yellow suit. Bumblebee shows me how to walk in heels.

"Slow down, Bumblebee. She got ass, but not as much as you, girl. Damn, Bumblebee, slow down, girl. That big black ass moving more than anything else," T-Red says, and Bumblebee laughs hysterically as she continues to prance in her own black heels alongside me in my yellow pumps.

"It's amazing how children grow so fast. You can't stop them from growing," T-Red says.

Soon, everyone goes outside to enjoy the cool breeze under the oak tree. Maymay, Bumblebee, and I are sitting under the tree, watching the children play stickball. I can tell, by the way, that Bumblebee is looking at me that I am going to get it for mouthing off to Maymay.

"Maymay tells me that you didn't want to wear them clothes that white lady had. That white lady wanted me to drop it off to one of them charity places, but I thought of you. Why do you want to look like a boy?"

I don't answer. I am cleaning and cracking the pecans that I picked from Mrs. Canoe's backyard with a hammer.

"Celeste, I told Maymay about the bathroom. T-Red and me had to put two and two together. Somebody been looking at his nasty magazines. I tell him not to keep them things in my house, so he put them in Maymay house. Somebody been looking at them. Maymay say that you been staying in the bathroom too long. She been listening to the pages turning. She been cleaning your clothes. She and me know you been doing stuff in there. T-Red know, too, but he can't say nothing to you," Bumblebee says.

I stop cleaning pecans. I want to get up and go, but where can I go? Who can I run to? Maymay looks at the children playing in the yard. I look at her for answers, but she looks straight ahead. She rarely avoids me.

"It's all natural, Celeste. You don't want to be like your mama, but you can't hide your womanhood. T-Red and me both think that maybe you like girls, since you trying to be like a boy. He says you trying to be one of them girls that like girls. You don't know it, but that is what Mrs. January is. When I go to Mrs. Leblanc's to cash my check, they tell me to tell you to watch Mrs. January because she one of them people from California who likes women. She an old bull dagger. They trying to get her out of that library. Mrs. Leblanc told me that she and a lot of people around here never even met a same sex person before. I think that's the right way to say it. We not like that, here. We all want to have babies and husbands and continue our bloodline. Did you know that the devil was a homosexual? Did you know that? Maymay told me about that African dress she had. It don't show you as a woman. I gave it to T-Red. He gonna tell Mrs. January where she can put that dress," Bumblebee says. She looks for a reaction from me, but I am so shocked that I can't say anything. A lonely and warm tear makes its way down my cheek. For the first time, I show them my pain.

For the first time in my life, I hate Maymay, who looks out at the horizon of partially cleared sugar cane fields. Her eyes are searching for something. I think she is looking for my pain. She wants me to feel pain. She knows more than the others about me. She knows I love to read. She knows this because of all the times I've helped her cut okra, clean fish, can blackberries, and washed her dirty clothes. She knows I always asked her if I can read now. She makes me so fucking sick. I want to hit her with this hammer in my hand, and I've never felt this way before. Reading helped me to escape from T-Red and Bumblebee's hell. Now she wants to take this away from me. And how dare she invade my privacy by listening to me? She is so mean.

"Mrs. Canoe does not live here anymore. She's at the old folk's home. You haven't been going to church anymore with her. Maymay wants you to go to her Catholic church only. She wants you to make your confirmation. She will sew you a white dress. Maybe the children can go to the Catholic church, if Father sees how you know so much about God. I am not Catholic anymore, but both Maymay and me think you need to be in somebody's church to keep the evil spirits away," Bumblebee says. But I am not paying attention to her. I am paying attention to Maymay. I stare at her hoping she will feel some guilt.

The glaucoma is now taking over Maymay's right eye. I think of Mom Dot and her blind evilness. I want Maymay to say something, because I know she knows how much she has hurt me, but all she does is stare at that damn pretty blue sky with her evil eye.

Chapter 16

The Curse of the Mulatto

Celeste

Maymay tells me before I leave with Liver, "I know Mrs. Canoe is at the hour of her death because that big owl has been hooting his ass off all night."

I see the owl in the back yard through the kitchen window when I am washing dishes. It is a beautiful bird with wide, aware eyes. It seems that the owl knows so much more than we all do. The owl, like Maymay and Bumblebee, finds every hidden secret. As it flies over us at night, its colossal wings cast a great enveloping shadow over Maymay's small, sharp shoot Creole house. The full moon and the back porch light, which Maymay claims helps keep the Black Fuckers away, helps create shadows and mysteries among us all.

The owl's big beautiful eyes mesmerize Maymay as it perches on the post of the clothesline and stares at her. Staring past the familiar owl and looking at the moon, Maymay comments, "There is a full moon, so a baby must be coming. Bumblebee pregnant again. Must be her. That moon never lies."

That is the only old wives tale I believe, because if the moon can affect the tides of the water, it would follow that it can affect the human body which is about 70 percent water. Many of Bumblebee's and Mama's children are born at or before the full moon.

I can time my and my sister's periods according the full moons. Maymay says that when the girls are around each other, their periods affect each other.

That night, I go to bed. I have learned to wrap myself with a quilt so that Tiny doesn't wet me, especially since Maymay is listening to me take baths now. I don't stay long in the restroom, and I am dressing more like a girl, as Maymay wants me to.

Before Maymay goes to bed, she tells me, "I want you to start seeing boys. Bumblebee is so nice. She says that you can invite them to her house. You can also use her phone. She says that too many girls get hot when they go to college because they don't get to live their life. I want you to invite that little boy who always asking about you in town. I know his people. T-Man used to spot cane with his granddaddy. I don't want you going to college not knowing how to act around little boys." She closes the door to our room.

That morning, I am excited about the train ride. Catching and riding the train is one of the most exciting things I have ever been allowed to do. I stare out of the train car and everything whooshes pass me. It is hot outside, but sitting in the open boxcar gives me and Liver a relaxing breeze.

We are the only ones in the car until we see Yankee Doodle with his scraggly beard and work clothes running trying to hitch a ride on the boxcar. Liver helps him up, and he hops in the car. He has a burlap sack with his belongings.

"Hey dare! What y'all say?" He has an open mouth with only four rotten teeth, and he smells like cheap corner store liquor. I learned that you can keep your teeth white by using baking powder if you don't have toothpaste. And a towel if you don't have a toothbrush. "There is no reason not to brush your teeth," Mrs. Canoe would always tell me.

I keep silent and begin to read my book. Liver begins to eat the food in the brown paper bag. I fixed my fried chicken, bread, macaroni, and Moon Pies for dessert.

Yankee Doodle stares at me. "You show is a nice looking yeller gal. Your hair is so pretty and long. *Mais*, look like I seen you already somewhere before. Where I seen you at?" There is a long pause as Yankee Doodle looks at me.

Yankee Doodle's voice explodes and his expression holds the familiar look of Belle Place residents. "Tut! You Tut daughter, la *passé blanc. Mais,* dat's a big *petain.* Tut pretty, but *petain*," Yankee

Doodle's laugh is thunderous and overwhelming. And he now shows me all of his rotten teeth. His breath stinks, and I cover my nose.

Liver does not address Yankee Doodle's personal conversation. He is there to make sure that I make it safely to town. He eats his chicken and minds his own business. He whispers to me, "If he comes in our space, I am going to clip him. Don't worry."

"All y'all crazy back dare in dem woods. You got that crazy Mulatto blood." His eyes drift as he recalls a familiar story: Virgin Mary needed to save her baby. "Rode a mule—one of y'all mule-lat-toes. She cussed that stubborn t'ing!" He bursts into hilarious laughter. Taking the burlap sack from underneath his rear, he places it underneath his head. Stretching in the corner of the boxcar, he takes a nap. As he wiggles around to get comfortable, he just keeps giggling and whispering, "She cussed that Mule. Cussed it. Cussed that t'ing. Heee Hee Hee."

Suddenly, there is a change in his tone and mannerism. It is no longer a joke to him. He is serious. He rolls his eyes and looks off into the distance to some faraway place. Angrily, he rolls his eyes and shouts, "Cursed dat t'ing!" He looks at me with wild crazy eyes, as if I must believe him or die. "Cursed dat t'ing!"

It isn't the first time I have heard that story. I once asked Ms. January if she had any books about it, and she said, "That's an old etiological tale. It isn't real. It is just a story that people use to explain something that happens today, like why the sun sets. It is a story that tells how the Mulatto got its name. It is not true. The Virgin Mary didn't curse the Mulatto. Why, I'm Catholic. Even I know that."

I am still unsure, because T-Man tells me the story, too. After T-Man tells me the story, he looks at me the same way Yankee Doodle looked at me. T-Man said, "The Mulatto is cursed. They owned a lot of land, slaves too. It was all stolen by the white man after the big war when ditches on the side of the road were filled with hundreds of dead men and their blood flowed through the ditches like water."

Mrs. Canoe doesn't believe the story. "God and the Virgin Mary both have mercy and would never curse his children."

I even look in the big unabridged dictionary in Belle Place High School one day. The origin of the word is mule. I feel that it has to be true. Why would the story fit so closely together?

"He is going to miss his stop," Liver says.

"He doesn't care. All he cares about is that old whiskey bottle. I hope he ends up in Canada and doesn't come back for making fun of us," I whisper and chew my fried chicken.

"We are almost there. The old folk's home is about a mile from the tracks. We can walk there," Liver says. Liver makes me jump first because he is scared that I wouldn't jump if he jumped first. After I jump, he jumps. We jump by the sugar cane fields so we don't get in trouble with the law.

High in the sky, the noon sun shines merciless hot and bright. Dark rain clouds are also in the sky. Far in the distance, a tractor is cutting a patch of cane. Blowing in the wind in front of the cane are dandelions in November. I think that this is strange. Liver and I walk together in the heat for a mile on the hard limestone gravel of the tracks and then on the hot blacktop road for another mile to get to the old folk's home.

Soon we reach the home. Mrs. Canoe lies in her bed. The room smells of medicated vapor rub. Propped up in the bed by three pillows, Mrs. Canoe rests with her eyes and mouth open. Her head slowly turns as she hears the light tap on the door. The nurse tells me that Mrs. Canoe can still hear and understand everything they say, but she can't talk. I am so happy to see her.

I take out the plate of food that I cooked the night before and placed in a paper bag. I have all the things that Mrs. Canoe likes. I made sure that everything was healthy when I packed it. There is baked yard chicken and smothered okra from Maymay's garden. Mrs. Canoe loves yard chicken, especially the feet.

I say, "Good afternoon. I miss sweeping and mopping your house, dusting, fixing your beds, washing your dishes. I even miss emptying out your toilet pot. Everything is nice here. You don't need me to help with your chores, but I can do my last and final chore, which is to read you your *Bible*." I read the twenty-third Psalms, Mrs. Canoe's favorite.

"Let me tell you what's been going on our street. First, my mother has a boyfriend now. She lives with him in Sunset. She met him about a week ago. Maymay has all the children. Even though I can't come by you anymore, my mama left me a secret place to go to. I had to give it up because Maymay says the men who have been working in the fields were getting closer to it. I might get chopped up. It has been torn down, now. She says there are men who hide in the sugar cane. They are running out and trying to find somewhere else to live. They are dangerous. She says she saw three of them yesterday," I say. Mrs. Canoe seems to be listening quietly.

"I love the Big Chief tablet Mama left me. I write my poetry in it. Mama wrote a lot of Diana Ross songs in it. I am not going to tear them out of the tablet, because she will be too upset. I pray and dream, just as she did there." I say.

Mrs. Canoe shakes her head and looks long into my eyes.

"I remember what you told me. I know that just because Mama made mistakes, I don't have to make them, too. I hold everything dear to my heart. I found me a prayer I can say on a card in my mama's box. I want to read it to you. If you look at the picture, it has a path that looks just like the path to our house." I read the serenity prayer.

I stare at the picture. I say, "Mama's catechism teacher gave it to her. It's not Baptist, and it's not Catholic. It just expresses everything that I've been through in my life." I hold on to Mrs. Canoe's hand and lay down on her breast and cry and rock back and forth.

This is the last time I ever saw Mrs. Canoe. I ride the train back to my home. The sun is setting in the open sky. It has all the hues of dawn, even Virgin Mary Blue. I stand there in the open boxcar and stretch out my arm. I can feel the light drops of drizzle on my warm skin. I think about that word "bloodline" that Bumblebee used as I look at the visible veins in my wrist. T-Man, Maymay, and Mama, all flow through me just as the train flows alongside that muddy Bayou Teche that flows through New Iberia, Belle Place, and Sunset, where my mama swings with wild and flowing hair.

I remove the unsightly rubber band from my hair. It pops and stings my wrists. I run my fingers through my greasy, pressed hair, and my hair freely flows. My hair floats like the wind and the strange November dandelions.

The tractors are riding back to where they belong. The egrets are done searching the fields for worms. I inhale the cool, wet air like Maymay inhales her pipe when the last of the tobacco is gone. I watch the dandelions float in the November sky. The sky is blue and black now. The dandelions look like snow. I think about when I was born. There were light flurries of snow in Louisiana. Everyone knows it never snows in Louisiana. Well, it snowed on my birthday. This is some strange sign, I think.

My mother tells me that when the sun is out and it is raining, the devil is beating his wife. Maymay always disagreed with Mama. "She would say, '*Non, non* it don't go like that. It mean God is blowing kisses at you." Maymay and my mama would look up at the sky as if it were a miracle. I have often observed this supernatural occurrence in the open, vast sky. Well, today the sun is out with the light rain and blowing dandelions that look like snow. I know it is a sign from God.

This is my cleansing rain. It is a gift from God, just like my life is a gift. Only these light flurries will cleanse me from my mother's bad reputation and the curses on my family. It shows that I am truly born again, like Mrs. Canoe says I am. The Virgin Mary is with me, too. That's why the sky has Virgin Mary Blue or pure blue. I stretch my arm out to feel the drizzling rain and the smooth vibration of the train. The train picks up speed. I move my arm from the stinging rain and wind.

I drift into a deep, deep daydream among the floating dandelions and rain that has soaked my body. My hair is soaked, but I don't care. The rhythm of the train calms and soothes me as nothing has before. I rock softly back and forth. Again, I have hope.

Chapter 17

Extended Time with Spirits in the Walls

Celeste

"Look how Canoe just passed away out of nowhere. I don't care if'n this tobacco is too high. I'm going to smoke my pipe all I want," Maymay says. "I am going to enjoy ma living while I'm still on earth. I can watch *Star Search* in peace. I don't have to worry about that narrow ass girl twisting in front of ma TV hollering about people singing her songs. I am at peace."

"I like the new time. We have longer nights. I have more time to spend with my dead people. Not all of them come back to me. Ma Aunt Tont, ma sister La Lest, but not T-Man. He probably found an old lady out there. Ma mama once told me you have to give dead people they time. He probably feel I'm not ready yet," Maymay says. She is staring eerily at the wall across from her bed. I stare at the wall with her, hoping that I can find a spirit or two.

The tulip lamp casts a shadow on my Maymay. She looks pretty and nice, not like she did the day under the tree when I cracked pecans with a hammer, and she told everyone my secret of looking at naked pictures in the restroom. No matter how much I hated Maymay that day, I can't stay angry with her. She is my Maymay.

"Maymay, did you know that my mother had a house in the sugar cane? She kept a box with a lot of things from her past. All of her stuff was in a metal box like the lock box that you and T-Man had. She told me to go there and get the box. I would like to see my mama again. Maybe I can give her the box whenever I see her again. I would like to put the box in the attic, if it's okay with you," I say.

"Yeah, they about to finish cut the rest of them cane. The Black Fuckers are gonna wait until next year when the cane is high to attack little, pretty girls like you. I guess it would be okay. I didn't know that girl was going in and out of them cane like that. I would see her walking back there, but I didn't know she had a house in there. I can see if that was one of them children doing that, but she's a grown ass woman with four children. She's running in the cane like a crazy woman. I been to Pineville once before, and I ain't never done nothing like that before. I'll be damn," Maymay swears as she takes another puff from her pipe. She gives the wall a long, intense look. I imagine that her sister and her are having a mental conversation.

"*Mais*, you give me the stuff. I'll put it in the attic." Maymay examines the old locker box that I hand to her. "T-Man had this in the trash pile. Tut must've took it out of there. *Mais,* look, she even wrote a letter and taped it on the front of the box." Maymay tries to read the writing on the metal can.

"I wrote that, Maymay. I thought that it would give the younger girls and me hope since Mama is off somewhere with Black. This box is all she left us, her children." I say.

"*Mais,* I know you're not crazy. You bring A grades home without studying. You always got a book in your hand and use words no one in Belle Place knows. I'm going to let you put her stuff in my attic, just you. I wouldn't let anybody else do that. It's grinding time now, but maybe next time you can have a little place in the cane." Maymay laughs. "You would have to get it closer to the house, 'cause I don't want nobody messing with my baby."

"You can sleep with me in ma room if you want to and read your *Bible* next to the lamp at night. I'll feel better knowing you next to me at night. T-Red helping out at Cajun Sugar Mill since it's grinding. There's no men folk back here with us. This is a small town, and T-Red say boys always asking him about you. They're too many eyes on you, Celeste. Those men miss Tut. They want the next best thing," Maymay says. She smiles at the wall and waves hello.

"I don't want anybody peeping at you at night. I got ma gun here. I'll shoot them dead if they take you from ma bed," Maymay tells me as she continues to smile and smoke her pipe.

"I would like sleeping with you, Maymay," I say. I get into the bed with Maymay.

"Don't you wear night clothes, girl? I sewed Tut a lot of nightclothes. She got a whole drawer full. You the same size as her, now. Put her clothes on," Maymay says as she gets out of her own clothes to put on a nightdress. She removes her pink housedress. She is not wearing a bra. Her breasts are flat and wrinkled. Her body is frail and saggy. I think about my mama as a baby, sucking on her breasts, and I feel weird.

I feel uncomfortable watching my grandmother. I've seen my mother undress many times, and I never felt uncomfortable. I think it's because Maymay's body is so unlike my mama's and mine. I want to sleep with Tiny, who still snores and wets the bed, but I think about the soothing lamp and the cozy quilts. Besides, Maymay's shotgun will protect me from the lustful men and boys who miss Mama. These are the men who want to call me a whore and keep me in this shit box of a town.

"Maymay, Please tell T-Red to tell anybody who asks about me that I have a boyfriend. Tell them that I am engaged. Please tell them anything," I tell Maymay who is now in bed, adjusting her radio. "What can I tell them to make them stop asking about me? I hate people in this town and especially the men."

"Celeste, you never answered me and Bumblebee. Do you like women?" Maymay asks.

"I don't think that I do like women, Maymay. I confessed to Father that I like to look at naked pictures, and he told me it is probably because I see things in those women that I see in myself. He doesn't think that I am homosexual. Or gay, is what he called it," I say.

"That's all I wanted to know, Celeste. We just wanted to know why you was looking at those naked pictures that T-Red got, cause he say none of them men. I made him get rid of all of those pictures in the house," Maymay says.

I am trying to grab bugs that are flying in the light. "I know that I am not gay, because I think that I am in love with someone. It is not a woman or a girl," I say. Maymay now lights her pipe.

"Be careful, Maymay. Remember that T-Red says that you can burn the house by smoking in the bed," I say.

"Did T-Red buy this damn house? Him and that black bitch must want ma house and the rest of my land. Who you in love with, gal? That's what I want to know," Maymay says. She places the lit pipe in her mouth and smirks.

"Can I be honest, Maymay? If I am going to sleep with you, I want to know that I can tell you anything. I want to know that you don't really hate me. I want to be able to talk to you like I was able to talk to Mrs. Canoe," I say.

"I promise. I won't get mad, Celeste," Maymay says.

"Well, after I spoke with you and Bumblebee under the tree, I was really hurt Maymay. I was hurt because people in this town are so mean to people who know how to think for themselves. They don't like change or people who are different. Ms. January is smarter than any of my teachers. She is smarter than anyone I know. She holds book studies in the library. After school, I go to the library and read. Most of the time, we close the library together. She brings me home, because I hate riding that stupid bus," I say. I stare at the tulip lamp and watch a bug that is flying in circles. "The next day, I went to the library, and I apologized about the dashiki."

Thankfully, T-Red didn't curse her like I thought he would. He still thinks that he has to act different in front of white folks. I told her that I was still going to wear the dashiki and the *tignon*. When T-Red took me to the speech and debate competition in Lafayette, I brought it with me in my big purse. T-Red would never look in my purse. He has this thing about looking in women's purses. I had my hair pretty and curled. Bumblebee did my make-up, and I wore the yellow suit that you tailored for me. I hated the suit and the pumps. I tried to avoid the looks and the stares.

For a moment I leave Maymay, her spirits, and her extended time. I am at the speech and debate competition. I am wearing the yellow suit and the yellow high heels. I am holding the dashiki and *tignon* in my hands. I am trying to rush to the nearest restroom.

Suddenly, I hear this rich voice. It is a voice with a beautiful accent. It's nothing like my Frenchy accent that I despise. The person sounds so passionate and strong. I can only imagine what he looks like.

The voice is coming from an open door. I take a peep in the door, and there he is. He is dark and muscular with skin as smooth and as dark as a Hershey bar. His hair is twisted and exotic. I've never seen hair like his before. His beautiful, handsome body matches his rich and passionate voice. He is reading about early love in a poem called "Adolescence." He speaks about late afternoon and four-o'clock flowers closing and him sleeping half-naked. It was a poem about nothing cooling his fever.

Well, I knew from the moment that I laid eyes on him that nothing could ever calm the feeling I felt in my body for this young man. I fell in love with the poem and him. I felt a quiver in between my legs, and I had my first orgasm without touching myself. I memorized the poem.

When he is done, I know that he feels me. He feels my passion as much as I feel his. He turns and looks at me, and I look at him. We look at each other like we knew each other. I feel like he feels the passion I feel in between my legs when he speaks in his rich accent.

He looks at me, and I want him to look at me. I want him to find each curve and every nook and cranny that Maymay's needle found that day she altered the yellow suit. I no longer want to change into the dashiki. I want this dark human being with his dark bright eyes to look at me. I want him to like what he sees. We just stare at each other. We own this space and time.

I check my paper with my room assignment. I am in his room when his group is over. He comes to me, and he says hi. I say hi to him. He takes a seat in the back to watch the next group of speakers.

I am supposed to read "Ego Tripping," and I am supposed to read an essay that I wrote on the *tignon* and how Black women were made to cover their wild exotic locks, but I ask the judges if I can change my poem. They say that I can, and I do. I recite the poem, "Renascense" by Edna St. Vincent Millay.

When everyone is done, he meets me outside, and introduces himself. "Hi, my name is Vashan. What's your name?"

"My name is Celeste. I really like that poem you read."

"It's 'Adolescence' by Claude McKay."

"I read 'If We Must Die,' but I never heard 'Adolescence' before. It's really beautiful. I really enjoyed it. You have a really nice accent."

"I am from Jamaica, just like McKay. Do you want to go for a walk? The University of Southwestern Louisiana is a pretty campus."

I don't want to get in trouble, but I am almost paralyzed by his voice and his handsome looks and beautiful white smile. He almost seems like an angel and not a human being.

I say, "I would love to."

I stuff the *tignon* and dashiki in my huge purse. He is such a gentleman. He holds my hand and opens every door for me.

He takes me to his car so that we can sit and listen to reggae music.

"My father knew Bob Marley. He died a few years ago. We went to the funeral."

"I like the music. It's very different," I say. It kind of reminds me of zydeco, because it's so different.

"Where are you from?" he asks me.

"I'm from Belle Place, Louisiana. I live around a lot of sugar cane fields. There isn't much to do there but look at the big, blue sky. The sky takes over everything. I look out the window, and all I see is the sky and the sugar cane," I say and laugh. "I guess that's why I like 'Renascense' so much. The sky is not so grand. I almost can touch it with my hand."

Vashan says, "Let's try something."

He opens the car door on my side and lifts me up with his strong muscular arms. I tell him to put me down, because I feel that everyone is looking at us. He places me on the hood of his car. The hot hood burns my legs that show through my slit. I kick off the high heel shoes. He snuggles next to me. He smells so good. I just want to bury my head in his strong chest. He wraps his big arm around my neck and grabs my arm and holds my left hand.

"Let's touch the sky."

He holds my hand and writes our names in the sky.

We listen to more music and talk some more.

He looks in my eyes and sings "Redemption Song" to me. I stare in his eyes. I want to kiss his full, brown lips. This seems like a beautiful dream. He continues to look at me with those beautiful, bright eyes. He moves over to kiss me. I feel my body erupt into electrical charges. I am so scared that he is going to take me somewhere I can't go with everyone walking pass us.

"Well, I better go. My Uncle T-Red will be looking for me. I want you to have my address. I like to write. I can write to you." Bumblebee always tells me to give boys my information but don't take theirs. If they like you, they should contact you, she always says. I really, really like him, but I don't want to seem loose like my mama by taking his address and writing him first.

I don't worry about him not writing me first. I know through his eyes, laughter, and the wet kiss that he leaves on my hand like I was something delicate and precious doll that we have fallen in love underneath the pretty, blue sky on the hood of his sports car, and he will find a way to get to me again.

Soon Vashan and all of the beautiful spirit of that day evaporates back into Maymay's wall.

"What did T-Red say when you got back to the car?" Maymay asks.

"He wasn't angry. He was listening to his music on his jam box. He was talking to the female custodians. He was telling a whole lot of dirty jokes. I don't think that he was too concerned about me. Everybody thinks I am perfect," I say. I turn and rest on my back now. I see Maymay from the corner of my right eye. She's angry and that startles me. The spirits of that day have vanished from our wall for good now.

"Nobody is perfect, Celeste. I don't know who put that in your mind. It damn sure wasn't me. Make sure that you don't go telling Father all your business, and I know I made a promise to you, but you better not ever disobey me again. You lucky you didn't wear that African suit because T-Red would've rawhide your little ass. I am glad that you like somebody, but he lives too far from here, and if he knew how poor you was and who your mama was, he wouldn't mess with you. Rich people not like us, Celeste. They think we got the same things like they got. When they see we don't, it's hard for them to believe. He would just use you," Maymay says.

I don't care what Maymay says. She doesn't know everything. She doesn't know that Vashan writes to me. I get the mail, and Maymay never sees my letters. He wants to visit me, but Bumblebee, T-Red, and Maymay will never let me date a Rastafarian with dreadlocks

There are no rooms like Maymay's. It gives me special feelings that no other room gives me. She has a door to her bedroom with a doorbell that leads to the porch. She said that in her days, people would enter your house through the bedroom, because they wanted you to feel welcome. To get to the restroom, you have to pass all three bedrooms.

My favorite things in her room are the old, iron bed that is painted pink, along with the matching pink iron tulip floor lamp. I like to sleep next to it.

Maymay says, "I sewed thicker curtains to match that lamp. I know I smelled some strong cologne two nights ago. They cutting them cane, and that brings all of the people who been living there out to mess with us."

T-Red believes everything that Maymay says, no matter how crazy it is. He tries to make sense of whatever she says. If she would tell us that she saw Elvis, he would have to figure out how. T-Red believes her and buys a ceiling fan with a bright light, but I only want the tulip light. It is so special and casts a dramatic light for us while she tells me all of her stories. I sleep so much better in Maymay's room that smells like sweet, red roses, mothballs, and tobacco.

We never watch T-Man's outdated black and white television. We listen to the soft rock and country music station that plays on the radio. Maymay likes listening to the news in French.

I say, "You know that T-Red said that you don't have to listen to all of that Cajun music. He says that there is a Black station now. Every time he changes it, you change it back."

Maymay says, "Me and T-Man listened to that station together. They used to speak much more French. I miss speaking French with T-Man. This way I feel like T-Man talking to me or listening with me."

"I have four heavy quilts in the cedar chest in front of the bed just in case you get cold during the night. Just let me know, and I'll get one for you," I tell Maymay after we say our rosary together.

Maymay has great stories about Cushma and the old days. I ask, "Maymay how come I have never seen Cushma, and you see him and your dead kin all the time?" The tulip lamp casts a shadow on Maymay's tired face as she stares and whispers.

"Well, some people see them and some people don't. Cushma is a devil, and maybe because you always read the *Bible,* and you have God in you so strong in your heart, you don't see him," Maymay says. She smokes her pipe and stares at the ceiling.

"I grab one of my rosaries and pray when I see him," she says.

Maymay has a rosary on each post of her headboard. I know that something speaks to me and Maymay from the other side. I mysteriously knew that my mama was going to leave me when I looked at the lightening and heard the thunder in the sky.

"Maymay, do you think that one day I can be a nurse?" I ask. I really want to ask if I can be a *traiteur.* I don't ask that question though. No one talks about it anymore.

"You can be anything you want to be, baby. You are a smart girl. Tut never tried to make nothing of herself, but you can try to be better. You can do much better. Don't let nobody discourage you, *cher.* Now let me go to sleep I'm tired." With that, Maymay turns her back to me and goes to sleep. Soon she is snoring underneath the soft, warm quilt. The wind whistles outside.

I touch my face. It is ice cold. I snuggle towards the tulip lamp. It's nice and warm. The Eagles are singing "Hotel California." I sing towards the lamp like it is my spotlight and microphone.

I like this song. I find out from T-Red that it's a lovely, not lonely, place. I sing it again with the word lonely because I want Vashan next to me reading poetry and singing his Jamaican folk songs in the tulip lamp. I miss him.

I think about that day when we sat on the hood of the Honda Prelude convertible. The metal was so hot against my thigh, revealed through the split of the sexy yellow skirt.

In the middle of the night while I am sleeping, my eyes become wide, wide open. I feel like someone is here in the room with me, and I know that Vashan will find me.

Chapter 18

Bouchierie

Celeste

Everybody wants to have a party in the Bastille family now that Mama is gone. T-Red has been killing hogs just about every other week now. "The Bastilles were always known for their good cooking and parties," T-Red says. Everybody is eating boiled crabs and listening to zydeco and T-Red.

Food always brings the family together and so do our yearly traditions. Every year after Halloween, there comes All Saints Day when Maymay's people come from all over to paint the graves and put fresh flowers on the coffins of the loved ones.

Every All Saints Day, Maymay tells T-Red to bring her to the cemetery. Maymay and I always see other relatives in the graveyard paying respects. Later that day, we all go to Notre Dame Catholic Church in St. Martinville and enjoy the church fair. Maymay says the same thing every year, "Times have changed and things aren't like they used to be."

T-Red and the men are frying the crackling in one big cast iron pot on a campfire under the tree. In the other cast iron pot, they are boiling the crabs.

T-Red takes a seat on the wooden chair next to his son, Liver, and the other men. He holds a 40-ounce of beer in his hand. With his legs propped up on a bucket, he begins talking loudly to everyone,

"Y'all dressing up for Mardi Gras this year?" T-Red asks. "I don't know. Me and Frog been wearing that same costume for the longest.

I guess it's time to change it. Y'all remember when we could beat people for Mardi Gras? Now dat's all changed. You get in trouble now for doing dat," T-Red says, after taking the last gulp of beer.

"Mardi Gras ain't what it used to be. I miss the good old days when we really had fun. People liked getting beat for Mardi Gras, and we liked beating them. Maybe this year I can kill another hog for Mardi Gras. Tut old man, Black, called on the phone a few days ago. I spoke with him. He says he going to put his car in the parade. People don't fix up their cars like they used to, either," T-Red says. "The only thing that we don't need to change is the way family sticks together."

Chapter 19

Bloodline

Celeste

I am sitting at the kitchen table with Maymay. The horizon isn't as empty and lonely as before. It is full like the big crabs I am eating. It is full because my heart is full, full of love for my family and full of love for Vashan. I like the feeling of being with family and friends.

"Who is that woman who keeps staring at me in the corner?" I ask Maymay. I don't recognize Mom Dot because she has shades and a scarf on her head.

"That's Mom Dot. Bumblebee is mad that I invited her here. She say I should have left her with her cats. She say she going to bring her hoodoo here. She one of the few *traiteurs* left. She can tell you about your dreams, and she can give you teas and advice from her dreams," Maymay says.

I walk over to her.

"Hi, my name is Celeste. I am Maymay and…"

"T-Man's granddaughter," Mom Dot interrupts. "I am Mom Dot. I just see in one eye, I am trying to look at you to see how pretty you've grown. You've grown so pretty. So pretty. You are a pretty, pretty girl." She touches my hair and skin. She removes her glasses. She grabs my hands and closes her eyes. I loosen my hands and move backward.

"There is something about you that is different. I feel like T-Man here in this room with us," Mom Dot says.

"T-Man said you wanted to be a *traiteur*. He told me that you asked him a long time ago. You were young then. I laughed when he told it to me. Not too many children or people want that job. Maymay told him she didn't want you being a *traiteur*. You going to college," Mom Dot says.

"No matter where you go, this thing is in your blood. T-Man had a great-great aunt who could tell people about themselves just by looking at them or holding their hand or something they owned. She saw dead people. They would come and tell her stuff. She didn't seek them. They sought after her. That's all I wanted to tell you. I'm sorry if I scared you," Mom Dot says. She looks sad and far away now.

I hold her hand and say, "Thank you so much. I am so happy to have met you. I was only twelve when my grandfather died, and I didn't know he spoke about me. I guess Maymay was just trying to protect me. One day if the good Lord willing and if it's in my blood, I will use God's gifts."

I kiss Mom Dot. "I'll come visit you sometimes when T-Red brings Maymay to your house. I'll help take care of your cats and chickens or maybe read your *Bible* for you," I say.

I go outside to watch the zydeco contest. For some reason, I look at the road, and there I see the Honda Prelude moving closer and closer to Maymay's house. The car stops in the driveway. Vashan looks at me. I look at him. He is playing Bob Marley. He wears shades and a baseball cap. He doesn't try to come any closer. He only stares at me.

The next night, when Maymay and I say our prayers, Maymay tells me, "I think that you need to go live with your mama in Sunset, Celeste. I had you sleeping with me because I wanted to make sure that you did not sneak out like your mama did. I was too busy loving T-Man. I couldn't pay attention to Tut. You thought I trusted you. How could I trust someone who is so aware of her body that she would dare touch it when no one is looking?" Maymay says. She is not looking at me, only the tulip lamp.

"He came here, Celeste. He asked about you. He saw you sleeping on ma sofa with your little red dress from that trash bag that that little rich girl Bumblebee work for sent. I want you to go by your mama and figure out what you want. I want you to go, Celeste. I want you to find that mountain and that wood you talk about in that sky poem. I done sent your paperwork over yonder to your mama. You fifteen now, and you old enough and smart enough to take care of yourself," Maymay says as she continues to look at the light from the lamp.

I cried that night so long and so hard. I don't know if I am happy or sad. I just cry.

Chapter 20

Passion en Francaise

Celeste

Dear Celeste,

You are right. The skies are very blue above the fields where you live. It is very, very pretty there. I felt the love of your family as I watched the children play their childhood games and the women and men dance to their French music. I wanted to grab you and dance to one of those love songs.

Your life seems so simple yet so beautiful. It kind of reminds me of Jamaica where there are poor people who find happiness in simple things. I don't care how much money you have. I really think that I have fallen in love with you, your poetry, your compassion, your style, and your beautiful hair. You are like no one I have ever met.

I went to your house one day. I had to go through a lot of trouble to get your physical address because you had a rural address. I went to your house one afternoon and you were sleeping on the sofa. You had a form-fitting red dress, and your hair wasn't pressed. It was thick and wet. I imagined that you had been running through the rain because it was a rainy day. I thought about you listening to the rain on the hot, tin roof of your Maymay's house. I fell in love again with you and your hair. I've never seen any girl with your hair color before. Your face was in the sofa, and you were so sound asleep.

Your grandmother was rocking in her chair watching television. She was so surprised to see me. She said that she had never seen hair like mine before, and she seemed afraid of me. She touched my hair and my face like I wasn't real. I asked her if she would wake you up just for a moment so that I could talk to you and look at your beautiful face. She grabbed a gun and told me to get the hell off of her property. She told me that some sheriff named Picard has given the citizens of Belle Place the right to shoot anybody who is in their house unwanted. I told her that I would write to you. I screamed your name as loudly as I could. You did not hear me, my sleeping angel. You were sleeping and snoring like the beauty you are. I won't sleep sound like you again until I see you face to face.

Love always,
Vashan Smith

Maymay snatches the letter from me. She gave me the letter that she and T-Red found in the mailbox. She never told me about Vashan coming to visit me. She puts it in the envelope and places it in Tut's dream box. "Celeste, you are ma blood, but I don't want to have to kill nobody. I don't believe in killing people, but if this boy comes on ma property without ma permission, I *am* going to kill him. T-Red said he'll kill him too, because he got a wife and children to worry about. He came here riding in that fancy car and looked at you to tease me. Picard told Red I can't shoot him on public property. Says I got to wait for him to come on ma porch or in the front room like he had the damn nerve to do that day. I never told you about that day. Then I got this letter in the mail since T-Red start checking the box. He had the nerve to write this letter. This is too much for me," Maymay says. She is very angry.

"It's not about Tut. It's not about what this town thinks. It's about respect. This is about him coming on ma property like he owns the damn place just because we have less than him, with his snakes in his head and his little sunglasses. It's about him telling us that we poor and looking at us dance like we some *bities* on *Hee Haw*. It's about you being in love with someone who is not like us. I can't take all of this shit in ma house. If people don't respect ma house, they can't stay here. I mean that. I told it to Bumblebee before and meant it. Now I'm telling it to you, and I damn well mean it. The only thing is, you didn't believe I said what I meant like Bumblebee did.

"I thought the curtains would help. They didn't. I still smell and feel him here. Even when he not here, I feel he thinking too hard about here. He said he is not going to rest. You need to go meet your mama. I am not thinking twice about this," Maymay says.

I ask, "Why, Maymay? Why? I didn't do anything."

Bumblebee walks in. She has a brown paper bag.

"Maymay, the doctor gave me the birth control pills you wanted. He say that these should hold her until her mama takes her to the doctor," Bumblebee says.

I am confused. Why is Bumblebee giving me pills when she is so religious?

Bumblebee continues, "Don't look crazy, Celeste. How do you think Tut stopped having children? These same pills. I love Red, and Red always worried about you. He want you to go to college and make us all proud. A lot of girls popping up pregnant, now that times are changing. You going to make fifteen, next month. Then you'll be sixteen and off to college. Your school will be paid one way or the other, because Maymay saved a lot of T-Man death check money for you, and she got some more money from her son's death."

"What about Maymay? She needs somebody to help her," I say.

Maymay says, "Celeste, you do a lot for me, but Tiny the same age you were when T-Man died, and you started helping me out. She can help me. Most of Tut children can take care of themselves, and T-Red is going to buy a phone, dryer, and washer after grinding. I am going to use everything now that you'll be gone and ma water bill will be lower." Maymay gets the family's only suitcase. It is packed with my clothes.

"What about Black? What if he tries to make a pass on me like T-Red said? What if he doesn't want me around?" I ask.

"T-Red's been over there by Black. They both work with cars. Red knows Black pretty good. Black is scared to death of T-Red. He is kind of on the slow side. Besides, T-Red say you gonna stay with Tut friend who live down the street. Tut say she gonna pay for your food and give her money every month. T-Red say Black and Tut fuck too much in that trailer. He don't want you hearing them sounds and then have to look at them walking around half dressed. You still hot about that boy with that crazy hair, and we don't want to give you a reason to use those pills. Tut friend is going to take care of you. She got cats and a lot of books," Bumblebee says.

T-Red doesn't look at me. I can tell that he wants to cry. I have one very important question, but it's only for Maymay, "Do you hate me and my mother?"

"Too much passion," Maymay says. She pronounces it in French. "You sat in that room and read that story from your heart. What kind of person does that living with hogs, and cats and dogs? You and Tut don't belong here. This is not the place for you. This is the place for me and Bumblebee and T-Red. I lost a son to Belle Place. We all thought that he left and never wanted to come back. Bumblebee found the death certificate. It said suicide. Bumblebee called the army and they gave us some money. I am going to use that money for your school and for this house," Maymay says.

Maymay motions for T-Red to get the rest of my things. He goes dutifully. He still doesn't look at me; he only grabs my things.

"Celeste, be careful out there," T-Red says as he carries my things to the car. "Don't let nobody use you like they used your mama. I don't like the way that boy comes to my mama's house like he owns the place. If you smart enough to memorize a book, you better be smart enough to remember where you come from. Sugar cane fields and a grandmamma with a lot of honor." I know that she remembered the word from our conversations in the room.

Maymay goes to her room and locks the door that leads to the restroom, the door that leads to the porch, and the door that leads to the living room. I know that she is cleansing her soul and the veins that hold hers and her mother's blood.

Chapter 21

Dead Grass Underneath a Blue Sky With so Much Life

Celeste

What is my mother like away from Belle Place? I've never cuddled in the drafty room with her and talked for hours and hours like I have with Maymay. I know Maymay's love stories, ghost stories, and conversation with the spirits, but Tut Bastille, I do not know.

Black's house was once on three acres of land. Black and his wife lived in a three-bedroom house that his wife hauled off to her mother's property when they divorced. Black's brown and white two-toned trailer now sits on the place where the house was. He still calls her his lawfully married wife, even though they are divorced.

There is dead grass in the shape of a house. The dead grass shows us all that there was something there, now gone. His trailer is the last trailer in the trailer park that is owned by Black and his ten sisters and brothers.

Now Tut lives with Black. She is excited about having a home that she does not have to share with another woman. She can decorate it the way she wants. She can sleep as long as she wants, and she can take a long bath in the bathroom.

There are automobiles dating back to the '50s. The latest car is a 1982. Black sells cheap parts to people and fixes broken cars to make extra money. Spare parts line the fence that separates his property from the trailer park that he owns.

"Hi, Celeste!" Mama runs to me like a teenaged friend. Her hair is pretty and curly. She wears it in a side ponytail. She is wearing a pretty pink short set with matching high-heeled sandals. She gives me a big kiss and leaves a florescent pink lipstick smear on my face.

"T-Red told me that you took those silly plaits out of your hair and you are dressing like a girl," Mama says. "At first they were worried about you until that boy started coming by Maymay's house. I got you an appointment with the health clinic two weeks from now. Girl, they backed up with appointments. Everybody's trying to get the pill," Mama says.

"Excuse the house. Black and me are still on our honeymoon. I am going to go to the store to get some things with T-Red. Make yourself at home," Mama shouts as she heads for the car.

All of the mirrors and glass have fingerprints. Everything with a surface has dust or black or brown grime. I am surprised to find an engine is in one of the bathtubs, and when I put the light on in the kitchen, roaches scamper about. T-Man and Maymay never tolerated roaches in their home, even if it meant spraying diesel around their house to get rid of them.

I can understand why Black brought my mama here. It looks like he needs something to make him feel better. He needs someone to cheer him up. He needs someone who won't judge him. My mama is good at that.

The trailer smells like cars, gas, and dust. I begin frantically cleaning up.

I have my own room. It has a soiled mattress with two big holes and no sheet. The springs are popping out. There is a dirty saddle on a chair, and the room is filled with dust like no one has been in the room for years.

I thought that I would be living with someone named Flossy, but I guess that my mama wants to prove that she can be a mama. I don't want to be here, but I get busy cleaning the living room and bathroom.

After a few hours, Tut and T-Red are back with bags and bags. She has been shopping for both of us. She has a new pair of shades with butterflies that actually have real wings on each side. She gives Black a big guilty kiss on the cheek, because she knows that she has spent too much money.

T-Red asks, "How do you like Black, Celeste?"

I say, "He is really nice."

"I see you cleaned up. The place looks really nice, but don't let Tut make a slave out of you. All these years you talk about Bumblebee and me, and you just performed a miracle and did the most work in your life. I am going to be in and out of Sunset. I work in the salvage business part time, like Black. They got a phone here, and if you feel uncomfortable at any time, Tut got a friend named Flossy who lives near here. You can go there. She is more of a homebody and church lady. She a little slower than Tut. Tut works with her. I wasn't going to leave you here, if you felt uncomfortable. That's why I left you alone with Black for a while. I know a lot of niggers get with the *mon* to get to the daughters, especially with trifling mammies like your'n." T-Red dishes himself a plate of food that Black cooked while I was cleaning.

"It don't take a genius to figure out that if a man with a 400-pound woman with rotten teeth, five girls, and on welfare, it ain't the food stamps he want. That was my cousin Stanky on my mama side, the Mulatto side of the family. T-Nonc called for the men, and we ran that nigger clean out of fucking town. He too scared to come back even for Mardi Gras. He was messing with all them girls, feeling on them and shit," T-Red says. He pours himself a huge glass of Mama's Kool-Aid.

"That stupid bitch said she didn't see it coming. The youngest was ten. Some men like that kind of stuff. They hunt for it like I hunt for rabbits in the field, but I'll beat the fuck out of Black if he touch you. Now, if you want him to, that's another thing. You'll end up like Tut if'n that's the case. If you feel he looking at you the wrong way, call me," T-Red says. He drinks almost the whole bottle of Kool-Aid from a mayonnaise jar in one gulp.

"I miss this red Kool-Aid, Tut," T-Red laughs.

My Uncle T-Red has so much nerve that he can bluntly speak about Black in Black's own house. Black watches his John Wayne movie as though he is talking about someone else. T-Red eats the last pig foot covered with red pepper and washes it down with more Kool-Aid. He takes the remaining Kool-Aid in a milk jug to bring home.

Tut is going through the bags. She is in her own world of butterfly glasses, flip flops, plastic purses, perfume, and lipstick from the many bags from the dollar store. She says, "Can you believe that I got us all of this stuff for thirty dollars." She is not concerned about anything that T-Red has to say.

Once T-Red is done eating, he takes a bag from Tut. It is probably payment for all of his trouble. He looks at Black, kisses Tut, and says, "This is your daughter, Tut. She's only for you, nobody else. Remember that."

Chapter 22

Queen of the Night Sky

Celeste

When T-Red leaves, there is an awkward moment between Mama, Black, and me. Mama says, "Celeste, thanks for cleaning, but Black is going to have the house dirty again soon. I cleaned this place the first night I came here, and it got dirty again. I threw my clothes away, and he went in the garbage and got them. I told him I wanted all new clothes. I don't want anything from Belle Place. He gave me sixty dollars, and I used the money you had. I bought new clothes. It wasn't but three outfits, but I didn't care. I am working around here, and I'll have enough money to buy more. Those clothes have bad spirits on them," Mama says.

"I'll wear your old clothes. I don't care about spirits. I need more clothes anyway. Maymay packed me in a hurry. I know that she didn't get all of my stuff," I say.

We are talking to each other like Black is not there, but he joins in the conversation. "Tut, I really like you. You are such a pretty girl, and you really have a nice heart. You can really cook and clean when you feel like it, but I really think that you need to see a doctor to get some nerve pills or something. I think that if you can get some kind of pills it can help you. I told my wife about you, and she tells me that that is probably all you need, nerve pills.

"I won't feel all the way comfortable with you until you can get your mind right. I am really attracted to you, but when I see that mad look in your eyes and you start thinking things that ain't real, I get afraid and feel bad, and I want to help you. I doubt that I will remarry, but I might need you to help with my kids."

She isn't even listening to Black. She looks at the crawfish pond. "Tomorrow we'll go crawfishing. It is so fun," Mama tells me.

"Can Celeste and I go for a walk by the store? I forgot something important," Mama asks Black. Black gets up and turns the television off. John Wayne and his gun fighting disappear. "I know about you and Mr. Smitty and all them other men. I don't want you leaving this place without me knowing. I don't trust you will do the right thing. You are too wild. I don't want you on my phone or fooling with none of my cars. I want you in the house at all times. I'm going take my key with me and lock you in this house if I have to. I don't want no problems out of you," Black tells my mama.

Mama looks disappointedly at Black. She pouts and sits on the other sofa. "I didn't know you would be like this. You didn't tell me all of this in the fields. If I would have known what I know now, I would have stayed in Belle Place or at least took my box with me to keep me company. Now all my stuff been plowed away by some tractor by now." Mama says. She begins to tear up as she thinks about her box and Black's rage.

"Shut up." Black screams at her. "I don't care about no box. I took you out of hell. I gave you a chance when no other man would take you. If you gon' stay in my house, you gon' live by my rules or else. I mean that.

"I am going to fix my brother Weston's car," he says. He then begins to talk to himself in French. When he gets angry he speaks in French, and Mama doesn't know what he is saying. He walks out of the front door with his toolbox.

Mama sits on the sofa, upset. She tells me, "He just wants me for my looks and my ass. He doesn't care about my dreams. He lied to me in the fields." She hugs me and cries.

"I hope he doesn't lock me in here, too. Maybe I should go to Flossy's house," I say. There is a long pause, and I say, "I have something for you, Mama."

I place the box in my mother's lap.

I read the note on the top of the box: "There is a sense of continuity in spirit, love, and laughter as long as your children carry your dreams after your life."

Mama reads each word with me. She stares at the box. "You took good care of it. You didn't forget. You brought it to me. Well, seeing how you love this box so much and you wrote a poem about it, I want you to keep it. I lose things here, and Black didn't want me to bring it here. He'll probably get rid of it. Hide it," Mama says.

We just sit there. My mom is so soft. She smells good, and she is playing in my hair now. I see some photo albums that I wanted to look at while I was dusting. I take a photo album and begin looking at Black's perfect family. There are pictures of beautiful girls with perfect ribbons and bows and lace dresses. They smile, sometimes with missing baby teeth. There are pictures of Easter baskets, baby dolls, and lollipops. There are perfectly wrapped presents with big bows. There are huge turkeys and pot roasts all on a beautiful white table with lace runners.

That night, Tut sleeps with me and we talk about Vashan.

"What does Maymay think about Vashan?" Mama asks.

"She thinks that he is a spoiled rich kid. She wants to kill him if he has the nerve to come on her property again. She says that rich people think that they own the world. But they don't own her and T-Man property. She hates his dreadlocks. When I look at him, my blood rushes through my body, and I can fly in the sky. I feel like I can touch the sky. I told him as much in a letter," I say.

Mama kisses me on the cheek and hugs me. She feels my belly. "I can feel butterflies flying in your stomach," Mama says. We laugh.

"I don't care what Maymay says. I am going to make sure that you take your pills. Black gives me mine. I'll make sure that you get yours. If you stay with Flossy, she will make sure that you get them. She is really reliable. I don't want my man giving you your pills," Mama says. Mama smells like jasmine perfume.

"I love the way you smell, Mama. You smell like the night blooming jasmine that Mrs. Canoe had growing on her trellis." Every now and then, Maymay would let me stay after the streetlights went on, and I would steal away to watch them come out. It was really a miracle to me. It was one of my favorite things. She got the plant from an Indian lady that she worked for in New Iberia. The plant was special to Mrs. Canoe and me. She would smile through the window of her kitchen, and we would look at them together.

Mama cradles me and we drift away into a peaceful sleep with night blooming jasmine in the air. Suddenly, the lights are on. It is 2 a.m. in the morning.

Black is standing there with no shirt and cut off shorts. His dark, muscular body shines above me, and I am scared to death. I imagine that he is going to lock us up in a room filled with dust. I cover myself from head to toe. He tells me, "It's time for your mama to take her medicine."

He takes Mama out of my arms and room and slams the door. I hear my mother scream, moan, and groan. I cover my ears with a pillow.

I am dressed at 5 a.m. The rooster continues to crow while I pack.

Chapter 23

Flossy's Dawn Breaking Sky

Celeste

There are little puddles of water in some of the holes on the gravel road. It has been raining in November, and now it is warm again, like August and September. My beach slipper feet are thick and hot. Tut told me the night before that Flossy lives in the first trailer. She told me because I asked. I remembered everything that T-Red told me. He told me who to go to, but I had no idea where she lived.

The sky is showing its first signs of day. I can hear the first sounds of day, as well: running lawn mowers, horns blowing, big yellow buses with screaming children, and birds chirping. The horizon is similar to Belle Place's horizon at dawn, but there are no cane fields where the land meets the sky. It's flat prairie with soybean fields for miles and miles. The houses are the same, old and run down.

At the end of the trailer park past Black's junk cars is a huge pond. Not wanting to go to Flossy's house too early, I find a fishing pole near the pond and I spend most of the early dawn and morning fishing. I don't even know if she wants me there. It is about 11:30, and I have a bucket filled with fish. If I am going to her house, at least I can make lunch or something.

When I arrive at the trailer, I see a lady watching the stories with her door wide open. I can see her through the screen door. I knock on the screen door. At first, the lady ignores me. I say, "Excuse me, ma'am, I am Celeste. My mama, Tut, said that I will be living with you. I have my things, and I can work. I caught you some crawfish and fish. My mama was still in the trailer sleeping when I left," I say.

The dark woman talks about *The Young and the Restless*. She says, "That Victor is something else." She creeps next to the door. I can see her face. All I can hear is the television. I see her long, dark arm as she unlatches the screen door.

I imagine that she is not wrapped too tight or a little weird. She walks and talks slowly. "You can have some cold water and sit right here and watch the stories with me. You can't use my bathroom, though 'cause I don't let nobody use my bathroom. I got two bathrooms. You can use the one in the hall with the shower stall," Flossy says.

The trailer is really neat and clean. It smells a lot like Maymay's house: mothballs and coffee. She has a gold clock shaped like a chariot with roses in it. There are a lot of plastic flowers and pictures of Jesus, Mary, and various saints.

I sit on a maroon velvet sofa. I take the beach slippers off, because gravel is stuck in my feet, and the rocks on the bottom of the beach slippers feel like little tacks.

"Don't take your shoes off on my rugs. You might have the fungus," Flossy says matter-of-factly. She turns and gazes into the television set and rocks softly. She is watching her stories on a 19-inch television set that sits on a wooden table covered by a blue and white crocheted baby blanket. Even though she has an air conditioning unit and fans, it is steaming hot in the trailer.

I am used to living without air conditioning in an old cypress house with high ceilings and occasional drafts, but as Bumblebee says, trailers keep the heat like the silver and black Thermos bottles filled with coffee that T-Red takes to work every day.

Flossy has a Jheri-curl, with beads of sweat on her forehead. She has a red tank top with blue jean shorts, and beach slippers. She smells like activator, petroleum jelly, and imitation expensive body spray.

"My name's Celeste. I'm from Belle Place," I say.

Flossy just talks to the television. "Don't go in that room. She gon' shoot you. Stay outside. Damn, I'm gon' have to wait to see what happens tomorrow." Flossy gets up and turns the television off. She moves one of the three fans that is in the room and increases its speed.

"My name is Flossy. You don't need to know my real name. You can stay here. Your mama said that she registered you for school. You're missing school, already. You can walk to school; it's just a few blocks away. Or, you can catch the bus. Me and your mama stay here during the day. We sell cold cups, dinners, and other stuff. We watch people children, too.

"Tut said that you a good worker and you gonna help me work, especially during the summer and during the holidays. We sell fruit cakes and peppermint baskets for Christmas," Flossy says as she rubs her cat.

I am happy that the lady is finally paying attention to me. It seems that Flossy is the only stable thing about this whole Sunset situation. "You have a nice curl. My mom wanted to put a curl in her hair, but Ms. Anna Mae the only hairdresser in my town says that her hair is too good for that. She gave her some other stuff to make it curly, but my Maymay says it is too high. She tells my mama to use water and VO5 conditioner, and she can have curly hair like them people on TV," I tell Flossy. "Ms. Anna Mae is always messing up people hair, anyway. She forgets to put curl boosters and don't use neutralizing shampoo."

"There is no such thing as good hair. My hair is just as good as yours and your mamas," Flossy says as she takes some activator from a jar and begins to grease her hair, looking into the flower mirror on the wall.

"Don't think that just 'cause you look white and have white people hair, you can come in here and make me feel bad about my curl. I've been wearing my curl for a long time. I don't have to worry about combing it. I got bad nerves sometimes. I like to walk back and forth and around here. I see you like walking. You was walking around here early in the morning as soon as the rooster start crowing. I saw you walking and fishing. I'll fry those fish for us later. I cook early in the morning, so I can watch my stories and babysit. I guess you didn't want to come here too early, but I am an early bird just like you. I was watching you the whole time. I saw you. You walked pass my trailer then you went to back to fish," Flossy says. "Maybe we can walk in the afternoon when the sun be down after school." She puts the cap back on the activator jar.

Flossy says, "I've been working with Tut for about two months now, and Black just tells me hi. He never talks to nobody. He stuck up! They say he depressed because his old lady left him and took them two cute little children. She left him 'cause he was always working, and he never showed her no mind. He was getting too mean to her."

"Do you have a boyfriend?" I ask. I hope that she says no. I don't want to hear her and some man screaming at night.

"Me? I don't have no man 'cause none of them want to do right." Flossy stops for a moment to see who is walking on the street. She is waiting for Mama.

"I know you hear them. I don't like to go there because, even when I'm there, they make all that noise. I be mad. Last time, I started knocking on the wall with a stick. They have no respect, those two," Flossy says. She begins to rub petroleum jelly on her legs, which makes them look shinier and longer.

"That's what all men want. They want a little bit right away, which I never give, and they go on 'bout they business just like I expect them to. I want a relationship. I get disability. I got this trailer from my sister. She went and bought a house in town. It's a big brick house. She lives by them rich, white folks. Her husband works on the railroad. He makes a lot of money. I just stay here, watch my stories, and read my Harlequin novels. I mind my own business," Flossy says as she grabs her romance book from the coffee table. She opens it to a homemade bookmark and places it on her newly greased thigh.

"You like to read?" Flossy asks me.

"I do. I love to read. I don't like to read romances, though. I like to read the classics and foreign novels."

"So you don't read Diana Ross songs, like your mama. I can hear her now, 'Diana Ross took a lot of my songs. I got discouraged about it,'" Flossy says mockingly.

"How bad are Tut's nerves? Has she ever been to Pineville?" Flossy asks me.

"They dragged Maymay off to Pineville, but my mother's never been there," I say.

"Well, she needs to stop talking about Diana Ross around me. I don't want to hear that. I can't have no yeller girl going crazy around me. I got enough problems. People know me around here from selling my stuff and minding my business. Craziness don't go with my name. I've been in special ed before, but I ain't crazy. I have a good reputation in this town, which isn't hard to have 'cause people are good and mind they business," Flossy says.

"For someone who has been in special education, you are really level-headed," I say.

"I'm just a little slow and mean. My mama fought to get me a check on account I fought a lot at school, and I once jumped off a bridge. A white man saved me. His name is Mr. Raymond. I finally got the check after that. It's not easy to get a check no more. My sister teaches me to save my money and clean up. She takes me where I need to go. I know how to drive, but I don't have a car even though I'm 25," she says softly.

I say, "Well, I don't know how to drive, and none of the women in my family knows how either, but Mr. Black fixes all kinds of cars back there. Maybe Tut will convince him to get you a car."

"He has the last trailer. He owns the trailer park," Flossy says. "Well, he doesn't really own the trailer park. His family and all of them own it. They were fussing about the land when the mother died, so they decided to make everything a trailer park so that way they can all have money every month. It's sad the way Negroes fight over a little bit of land."

"I told my daddy to give the land to my sister because she is always taking care of the family and me. I'm happy with my trailer and my cats. I always sleep with my two cats on the floor. The cool air sinks. You can lie on the floor and read one of my books." Flossy has four huge pillows on the floor. She has spread a hand-made quilt over them. Two fans blow on high speed on the floor. Flossy dives belly first on the huge pillows on the floor and begins reading.

Next to the sofa is a wicker box filled with books and Ebony and Jet magazines. I grab an Ebony magazine.

I open the magazine. I've never seen a magazine filled with Black people like this. The only magazines that we ever had was *National Geographic* magazines with naked black women and men with cloth over their privates. We would always get them with bags of hand me down clothes from Bumblebee.

There is a Black lady with her hair swept to the side in a curly ponytail. It kind of looks like my mama's hair, but it's prettier. I want to fix my hair like this and go out on a date with Vashan.

"Can I have this picture?" I ask Flossy.

"Sure. You can have the whole magazine. Just let me read my book," Flossy says.

"You think I can fix my hair like this," I ask her.

"You are going to need some rollers and setting lotion. You can have mine. I don't need them anymore," Flossy says.

I follow Flossy to the back of the trailer. She takes the book with her. She hands me a Tupperware container with rollers and hair supplies.

"You can have all of this whenever you leave because it's just taking up space," Flossy says.

"Can I try to do my hair now?" I ask.

"Sure, use the sink in the kitchen," Flossy says.

"The only problem is, I don't know how to style my hair like this. Can you help me?" I ask Flossy.

Flossy says, "I'll do it if you promise to walk with me in the afternoons. I want to lose some weight by walking, but the men are fresh around here. I don't like to walk alone. Sometimes, I have to walk to get my supplies for to make cold cups for the neighborhood," Flossy tells me.

She takes her book and places it in the clothes basket with some other books and magazines. She walks to the kitchen sink and stands next to it.

"Your hair is so thick and wavy. You are going to have to use the hot rollers. You don't really need a press. What do you use in your hair?" Flossy asks.

"I usually wash my hair with Ivory Liquid and let it dry in a ponytail. I press it, sometimes. Maymay always buys Ivory because she can use it for a lot of things, and it doesn't ruin her hands. Her hands get sore from washing dishes."

"You have a lot of sores and dandruff." She scratches my scalp with her long uneven fingernails. "If I had pretty hair like you, I would take care of it. Not too many colored folks have hair your color. Did you dye it?" Flossy asks.

"No, that's my hair color," I say.

"A lot of people have good hair, but it's black. Yours is sandy brown, like Tut. It's so different."

The cold pump water feels refreshing in my hair. The trailer is so hot and humid. I wonder if Flossy knows that she has just used the expression "good hair" that she hates so much.

"It feels so good to get my hair washed by someone else," I say. "This is the first time that someone other than Maymay has done my hair." My neck is stiff as she leans me forward in the sink, but I don't complain.

Flossy conditions my hair two times. She then pulls me back and wraps my head in a thick, warm, blue terry-cloth towel. "My scalp feels good and cool," I say.

I am now sitting on the floor between Flossy's legs so that she can blow dry my hair. "Yeah, I have all kinds of stuff from when I used to get my hair pressed. I like my curl better, anytime." Flossy is sitting on the sofa and neatly places all of the hair supplies next to her. She is having fun fixing my hair. "Your hair reminds me of one of my Barbie dolls," Flossy says. You have hair like my PJ Barbie. It's light brown with yellow highlights. It's long.

"Yeah, I still play with Barbie dolls even though I am 25 years old. I also have Malibu Barbie, Skipper, Ken, many others. I buy a new doll every time I gets my check. I like dreaming, and brushing the hair calms me down kind of like rocking calms your mama down."

"We never could afford Barbie dolls. Maymay always made our dolls for us. She knows how to make all kinds of things on her sewing machine. I would like to play Barbies with you one day," I say.

"You gonna have to stay still and stop talking so much if you want this to turn out right," she tells me. "Stop talking. I'll play Barbie with you, but some of them I don't want you to touch. They are still in the box."

Flossy places the hot curlers in my hair and leaves them in for a few minutes. When the timer rings, she takes them out and styles my hair like the magazine picture

Flossy checks the time on the chariot clock. "Tut should be here soon. I got our two children sleeping in the back. They come every day. I better check on them. Sometimes Tut sleeps late, especially if Black is not working," Flossy says.

I feel my hair. The curls are tight and neat.

"Thank you for taking so much time with my hair. When Maymay does it, she rushes. I have more burns and bruises than anything. You made me feel so special," I tell her.

Flossy says, "When Tut comes, you better ask her about school. It's Monday, and I am sure you will have a test on Friday. We can go under the carport and eat cold cups. I don't like going to her house because Black told Tut that I wanted him one time. I think he did that because he doesn't want Tut to have anybody in his house.

"I sell cold cups to the children around here. What kind of cold cup would you like?" Flossy asks me.

"I would like strawberry," I say.

"Okay," Flossy says.

Suddenly, there is a knock at the door. It is Mama.

"You left so early that I forgot about school. Everything is taken care of. All you have to do is go. Amy will walk with you," Mama yells as she walks to back of the trailer.

"You can help make the cold cups and stuff," Mama says. She is now holding one of the babies and is now getting a bottle from the diaper bag.

Flossy and I sit on the wooden steps. Flossy has a small, purple cold cup that is in an orange and white Dixie cup. I have a large in a red plastic cup. Flossy can't keep the grape cold cups because those are her favorite. She eats those all day.

We sit on the steps underneath the carport and talk about hairstyles and about our hometowns.

"People fine, over here. They nice. They mind they own business. They not messy to me unless they talking mess about me in French. I don't understand too much French. I wouldn't know or care one way or the other. My mama talked French, but she never taught me how to talk it. She said it would mess up my pretty English. I only talk English. I only know a few words in French." Flossy says.

"Yeah, my Maymay is the same way," I say.

The children are out of school. We hear the big, yellow school bus ride away at the corner. The sound of turning gravel echoes down the small road. There are about six children.

"Let's go by the cold cup and candy lady," I hear them yelling. They run down the street in the hot afternoon. Flossy makes cold cups whenever it is sixty degrees or above. She has candy bars, popcorn balls, hot dogs, and other things. She has a table in her kitchen with a slow cooker and microwave oven for the warm food. She is ready for her customers.

A boy of about 10 years old is the first to get out a quarter at the steps. The others soon follow, running and out of breath. There are about a hundred neat plaits all long and well-greased.

"I want a red hot."

"I want a strawberry."

"I want a grape."

"I want a tutti-frutti."

The children all shout in unison.

"Ain't got no mo grape," Flossy says, as she opens the aluminum screen door to take the familiar orders. She comes back with a platter of cold cups along with a cleaned out butter bowl to put the money in. The children begin to suck on the cold cups like thirsty puppies. When the edges are loose, they flip them over. Flossy gives them value for their money. She places peppermints or fruit cocktail at the bottom of each cold cup. She charges a quarter.

"Anybody want anything else?" she asks. A chubby white girl with straight black hair parted down the middle comes forward.

"I want a hot dog, three chocolate bars, a strawberry cold cup, a lollipop, and a pack of taffy," the girl says. Flossy screams the order to Mama, who places all but the cold cup in a brown paper bag. The girl gives her a roll of quarters and begins to suck on the cold cup.

Flossy says, "Thanks. Amy knows that I collect quarters. I have a lot of quarters. I like the bicentennial ones. She lets me keep the extras. Her dad is a rich Indian man who owns a lot of soda machines." Flossy tells me. "Maybe you can help me sort all of them, and we can go to Ben Franklin and cash them in." Amy looks at

Celeste as she eats her chocolate and says, "Are you Tut's daughter? She told me about you. She told me to pass by for you this morning, but Black said that you were gone, so I left," the girl says.

I say, "Yes, I am Celeste."

"I am Amy," the girl says.

Tut says, "I had everything ready. I thought that you left with Amy. You know Maymay wouldn't have you here unless I had your stuff ready. You better go to school tomorrow, or T-Red is going to start some shit with me and Black. Red was asking about you this morning. I overslept. Black and me was drinking some gin. I can't take alcohol too good, because I never drank before I came here. Black likes when I drink hard liquor," Tut says.

"Um, I wonder why he want you to drink so much," Flossy tells Mama.

"Besides, Celeste, I thought that you were going to stay with me and Black. I was finally getting to know my grown daughter. We was sleeping together and talking about that boy you like, Deshawn. I told him that I was going to let you call him, and he was going to come and get you for a date," Mama says.

"It's Vashan, and I don't want to live with you and Black if he is going to run around the house half naked all the time and make you holler like Maymay's cats screaming under the house in heat. I feel like he doesn't respect me. I feel really funny listening to the two of you holler all night." I tell my mama.

"Celeste, first of all, that's Black's house. Second, I can't tell him when, where, or how to do it, and third, you are too damn deep. How does a 14-almost-15-year-old talk like you?" my mama says.

Amy looks at me and smiles. We all have an awkward moment of silence, then Amy says, "You be ready for seven, so we can walk to school. Tut knows that I don't like riding the bus because the black children make fun of me. They pull my hair and call me prejudice," the girl says.

"I know what it feels like to be different," I say.

"Miss Tut talks to me all of the time when she waits for Black on the steps. Your mother is really smart and nice. I like her. She babysits my brother and sister. She is like a mother to a lot of people in this trailer park," Amy says.

"Do you have a phone?" I ask.

"Yes, we do," Amy says.

"Maybe I'll come by to see you tomorrow after school and use your phone. I don't want to use my mama's phone, and Flossy doesn't have a phone. My boyfriend says that I can call collect. I will be ready for school bright and early," I say.

Chapter 24

Rastafarian Skies

Celeste

This morning, my mama, Flossy, and I are all there when Amy brings her little brother and sister. I am up at about 5:30, but Flossy was probably up at five, because I can smell Pine Sol from the freshly cleaned living room. There is also coffee brewing and oatmeal on the stove, as well as baked chicken.

There aren't that many decorations in my bedroom, only brown walls and a frame, a box spring, and mattress. Flossy is at her table eating oatmeal and reading the newspaper. She has a box of cereal and bowls for the children. Flossy has a cup of rich black coffee in a huge mug decorated with fruit. Her hair is tied in a purple satin scarf, and she wears a purple housedress with furry purple slippers. She drinks the coffee and watches *Passe Partout* on channel 10.

"You want anything to eat? I got some cereal, oatmeal, and coffee," Flossy says.

"No, I don't eat breakfast all of the time. Sometimes I'll eat a boiled egg. Maymay always cooked dinner so early, that I never bothered eating breakfast," I say

Flossy seems agitated by my comment. "Well, if we go walking this afternoon, you gon' need to eat something and get a lot of energy. I cook early, but I don't serve until 10."

She goes to her little cabinet and takes out a cute brown and white ceramic bowl and shoves it at me. I pour Cap' Crunch and milk.

Amy and I walk to school. The school is about four blocks from where we live. My teacher's name is Mrs. Smith. She tells me, "I looked at your transcript. I saw that you had very good grades. We are going to keep you on the right track in this school. Your grandmother and uncle called. They want to make sure that all of your grades will count here." Mrs. Smith tells me.

The librarian is nice to me. I visit the library after lunch to check out books about Rastafarians. I want to know more about Vashan, his mysterious hair, and his Rastafarian sky in Jamaica. This school has more books about Black history, probably because there are more black children in the school.

That afternoon when Amy and I walk back home, Amy says, "Do you still want to come to my house?"

"Maybe tomorrow," I say. "Flossy really wants me to walk with her this afternoon. I gave her my word, and she has been so nice to me."

Chapter 25

Are You a Treasure or
Are You Looking for a Treasure in These Sunsetting Skies?

Celeste

I am so surprised at how much money Flossy and my mama are making in this small town. Amy alone gives her $10 a day. They are making about $50 a day selling snacks and $500 a month babysitting. Flossy even babysits on the weekends. Flossy is always looking for her next hustle or way to make more money.

"Where are we going, Flossy," I ask while I suck on my grape cold cup.

"We are going to talk to Mr. Raymond to see if he will let me sell plate lunches to men working in the fields. Then I am going to cash in some of my quarters and buy stuff for my cold cups," Flossy says.

"I'm glad you're coming because I can carry more and that will be fewer trips I'll have to make. Sometimes Tut and me catch rides, but I only catch them from people I know. One time, an old Cajun tried to knock my teeth out by throwing a beer bottle at me. When a car passes, I get out of the way. I almost walk in the ditch before I let them run over me. We got to walk towards the traffic. They have drunk drivers and people who hate Black folks," Flossy says.

I watch Flossy's strong muscular body. She looks like a man with breasts and long hair, but she is a woman who moves faster than a 10-speed bike. Her skin looks like coffee with a little cream in it. It is the color and texture of a smooth, toffee candy. Flossy is a beautiful woman. I cannot understand why she isn't the queen of some man's night.

She has everything that a man wants. Unlike my mama, she is so neat and tidy. She saves and manages her money very well. She has her dishes neat in the strainer, unlike Maymay and me who would just throw them in there. She has the cups on the cup side and the dishes standing straight up. Her dishtowel is always folded neatly to dry. I want to be like her.

Every morning, she walks through the house naked.

Flossy tells me, "What's wrong? All women got the same thing? Don't they?"

Today, blue and red pedal pushers and a blue tank top cover her man's body. She is wearing see-through jellybean sandals on her strong feet.

Flossy has a purse that snaps around her waist and a big trash bag. She says that she puts everything in one bag so if she has to run from a dog she doesn't have to worry about losing anything.

The sun is setting now. There is a cool breeze. The tractors are just moving to their destination to the various fields to continue grinding and harvesting the cane. School children are in their homes now, completing homework or eating their supper.

The traffic is not too heavy, just bearable. Flossy has long lean legs that can jump over the ditch so that she can walk on the side of the fields. I don't want to fall in the muddy ditch water by jumping in my yellow dress.

We turn down a long deserted blacktop road with only two houses. Far away in the distance, we can see a little, rickety, red one-lane bridge crossing the Bayou Teche.

We keep walking towards the winding bayou. "I'm scared to cross bridges. I'm scared of that spooky, dirty brown water," I say. "I know a lot of children my age that got drowned in the Bayou. I don't know how to swim, and I don't play with the bayou or the water."

"I'll help you cross it. It was hard for me to cross it the first time, too. I'll hold your hand and walk with you. You can close your eyes. You'll get used to it."

I don't want to cross the bridge. I can see straight down to the muddy waters underneath through the red cracks.

"Oh, no way am I going to cross that bridge. It is scary. It looks like dirty ditch water; that's how come it fools a lot of people. They think it's not deep, and it carries them all the way upstream. My Maymay says it is deep with a lot of dead bodies on the bottom. That bridge is red, old, and rusty. One of these cracks is going to open wide, and I am going to fall right through one of them little holes," I say, and Flossy grabs my hand,

"Get away," I say.

The Bayou Teche is about twenty feet wide and it seems to go on forever as far as our eyes can see. Living near the bayou, we always have to cross the water whether in Belle Place or Sunset. On either side of the bridge is long grass. "Maymay says they got snakes as big as men in that water. I can't cross that bridge, Flossy," I say and I run.

"There is a first time for everything," Flossy yells. I can't outrun her. She grabs me. "Don't play around this dangerous bridge. You'll end up killing the both of us. I'll fall in the water for sure and you with me."

A car passes by us, clink-clanking over the bridge. "Okay, I'll do it," I yell.

"I don't want you behind me, though. You might push me," I say. I can't look at the water in the rusty cracks below me. Those dark waters remind me of that dark day underneath those 100-year-old oak trees and Mom Dot's unnatural sky. They remind me of Cushma and the spirit wall that Maymay smiles and waves at. They remind me of T-Red slaughtering hogs and the scream of the dead mama cat I threw in the Bayou Teche.

I close my eyes and let Flossy lead me. I hold on to her waist. "Did we fall through?" I ask. Flossy laughs. I walk as slow as I can. I open my eyes, and I can see where the old rusty iron is now black pavement.

"I did it. I did it. This is the first time I ever crossed the bayou on foot," I say.

We walk for another mile until we see the grocery store. Flossy shows me how to shop from the clearance basket.

Flossy says, "One day Tut asked me, 'Why do you need to use a trash bag when you can just take a shopping cart.' I said, 'I've never stolen anything before, that's why.' Tut said, 'Well, we won't be stealing it. We'll be using it every time we go back, and I can ride you in it and you can ride me in it when we get tired of walking.' Tut took a shopping basket before we headed home. I returned it the next day," Flossy says.

When we get to the fields, the field workers stand there and stare at the two of us. Mr. Raymond recognizes Flossy, climbs down from his tractor, and walks over to her. He takes his blue baseball cap from his head and wipes the beads of sweat from his forehead.

He is a white man with snow-white blond hair and blue eyes. He looks over at me and Flossy and says, "Who is the new girl you walking with?"

Flossy says, "That's Celeste. She just a little, old country girl from Belle Place, a place you would never hear about lessen somebody tells you the name. Ain't nothing much there but sugar cane fields, hardworking black folks, and redneck Cajuns like you." Flossy covers her eyes with her long lean fingers and a red sweat rag to block the sun and look at Mr. Raymond, who is lighting a cigar.

She continues, "I want to know if I can sell lunches to the men in the fields. I would give you a cut." Mr. Raymond looks back at the men who are still staring at us.

"Y'all gon' stop my men from working, especially if you come back with Tut. Believe it or not, some of these men know about her, small town or not. I can't lead my men into temptation. We have too much to do. We have too much work," Mr. Raymond says. He yells to the men, "Y'all get back to work or y'all can go back home."

"Well, I guess I'm just going to have to sell my cold cups and food from the trailer park," Flossy says. I look at Flossy, who looks very depressed at the bad news. She had her hopes up. She could have made a lot of money selling lunches and suppers to workers after school.

Mr. Raymond looks at me and asks, "Are you a treasure, or are you looking for a treasure in these fields?" I just look at his white hair that matches the dandruff on his blue work shirt. He looks down at me from the tractor, and it seems like he isn't a real person but a ghost from Maymay's wall. I've never seen an all-white man before.

"Bring your friend to my church, Flossy. A lot of these men in this field were once alcoholics and drug users until I introduced them to the word of God. Y'all come to my church."

"What kind of church do you have," I ask.

"It's non-denominational with all races. We love everybody," Mr. Raymond says.

"Look here. This is a buffalo head nickel. I collect these. If you can find the answer to my question, I'll give you the nickel and $20, and I'll let Flossy and you sell to the men, because I'll know you have your head in a *Bible*. I saved Flossy from killing herself. She comes here to pray with me and study the word sometimes. I'll see y'all," Mr. Raymond says.

Flossy shakes her head, "Well, I'll be. You and your riddles. I've never answered any of them before, and I know I won't answer this one. Neither will Celeste. I'll be listening to you on the radio this weekend. Have a blessed day," Flossy says.

"I have an idea how we are going to make more money now," I tell Flossy. "Maybe we can sell our dinners across from Rusty's. Rusty's is a small corner store that has a washeteria like Smitty's back home in Belle Place, but he sells more liquor than food. His food prices are expensive. He needs a little competition."

"We'll see," says Flossy." How are we gonna get everything there without a car?" She looks at me as though I don't have a clue or an answer to anything.

I say, "I think my mama had a good idea. We could get a grocery basket and even decorate it with signs. My mother knows how to draw really nice."

We walk back. I cross the bridge more easily the second time around. I help Flossy place all of the supplies in her refrigerator. The next day, when I return from school, there is Flossy with a basket parked underneath her homemade wooden carport.

Chapter 26

Tut's Sky

Tut

I was so happy to find the new grocery buggy. Celeste told Flossy that it was a good idea. I must be smart like my daughter. After I see it, I run like a jackrabbit to my old man, Black. I am going to prove Bumblebee, T-Red, and all of Belle Place wrong. Flossy has about $2,000 saved for me. I'm going to buy a graduation ring for Celeste and Christmas presents for the girls.

"Hey, Flossy! My old man says that he'll help us fix up the basket so that we can sell our stuff to people around here."

Flossy is happy. She smiles, which is something she doesn't do much.

I say, "We need a light ice chest for the cold cups, and we can have a compartment for a box of snacks and, of course, a place to put the money.

"I always keep the money in my bra. That's not gon' change," Flossy says.

"Okay, keep it in your bra," I say.

Flossy says, "We'll take turns rolling it, so neither one of us gets tired."

I say, "And I can get my old man to put a seat in the front so I can push you when I'm pushing it. We both don't weigh no more than a buck fifty." We laugh.

The next day, we head for Rusty's. I use Black's children's oil paints to decorate the buggy. I make us a sign: "Tut and Flossy's Mobile Sweet Shop." There is an ice chest for cold cups and soft drinks. I have a gallon of my famous Kool-Aid and lemonade in a clean milk jug. We have pecan candy, pies, and candy bars.

We park our basket underneath an oak tree with our folding chairs on the opposite side of Rusty's store. We know that Rusty won't let us sell at his washeteria. He has a huge "No Soliciting" sign. Celeste already told us what that means. We can't sell on store property.

Rusty points to the sign, and I yell, "This is public property. No one can make us move. Your prices are too high. This place can use another business."

We have our first customer. It is a lady on her way to Rusty's with a basket full of laundry. "What y'all selling and what's your price?" she asks Flossy. Flossy points to the freshly painted sign on the side of the basket. "Them go your prices right there."

"Good prices. Y'all cheaper than Rusty's, and you got pecan candy and homemade stuff. I love pecan candy," she says.

The lady places $20, three fives and five ones, in my hand. She spends all of it.

"Your prices are much, much cheaper than Rusty's. He has been cheating people all of these years. It's about time he gets some competition. I hope y'all make it. No matter how silly people may say you look, don't get discouraged," the lady says.

Flossy says, "I have to save one of these dollars as a first dollar. They say it's good luck. I'll frame it." She gives me half, and she puts her half in her bra.

She says, "Here, I know that I can trust you with holding your money. This is all your idea, and it is a very good one." After five hours, we make a hundred dollars. We sell everything, even the entire gallon of Kool-Aid. Flossy gives me $50.

I mail Maymay a hundred-dollar money order. I am going to mail her money every month. Maymay mails it back with a letter telling me to give it to Celeste. We want to buy a car, and I want to save my money to buy a doublewide trailer. I want to buy it cash.

I am going to shop in one of those fancy shops on Main Street, and I am not going to let anybody tell me that I can't afford it. I am going to take Celeste with me, and she is going to buy something brand new that no else has worn before.

We are going to dress like the pretty women in the magazines, and Maymay won't have to sew it for me. It won't be a cheap outfit from Dollar General. The next day, I tell Flossy, "I want to go to Main Street. You need to get your sister to take us. I need about $300."

Flossy says as she counts our money, "Why don't you get your old man to bring you? You're always talking about your old man this and that. Get him to bring you." She keeps her eyes on her records to not lose track of her figures.

I say, "I don't want Black knowing all of my business. He don't let me know all of his business about his wife. I want my people to see that I have my own place and how I can decorate and buy my own new clothes. Everybody has put me down so long, I want to let them see how I'm living now."

"Tut, you have a velvet Stevie Wonder picture, the same green waterfall clock, the same First Supper picture, and the same comforter set that I have. You even have a dish strainer like mine. I don't want to walk in your house and think that I am still in my house. You need to stop trying to impress people. Impress yourself.

"Okay, it's time for you to go now. I need to watch my news. Go meet your old man. I'll see you tomorrow. Ask him about that car we gon' buy from him. I almost got all my money together," Flossy says.

Chapter 27

The Rain Stick

Celeste

"This car is nice. I like it," I tell my mama.

My mama and Flossy have a Volkswagen bug. It's got "Tut and Flossy" written in bubble letters and a big yellow daisy at the top. Tut and Flossy is painted with little yellow daisies on it, too.

Amy says, "I think I saw a car like this on TV or something. That's probably where they got the idea."

There is just enough room for the two of them after they load their tent and supplies. They bought it for $500. It needs a lot of work. She wants all of those people who laughed at them to really laugh now she told me.

I tell Amy, "Everyone in Sunset has good things to say about my mama and her business. For the first time, I feel so happy and proud to be my mama's daughter."

After I eat my supper at Flossy's house, I go to Amy's house. Amy answers the door right away as if she is expecting me. Amy and her mother live in the nicest trailer in the lot. It is a year-old trailer. Everybody else's trailer is older. Her mother is pure-blooded Native American, like Amy, but Amy's brother and sister have a black father.

"What is that in your hand?" I ask.

"It's a rain maker. My mother is a Houma Indian. She got it from a garage sale. We like to collect Indian decorations and things," Amy says. She is shaking the rainmaker.

"You want rain in the fall? In Louisiana, it happens quite a bit, but we haven't had rain in a while. My Uncle T-Red says Indians have a lot of money because the government pays them. Is that why ya'll have a new trailer? T-Red said that we have to show that we have Indian in us so that we can get a lot of money from the government. Maymay's great-grandmother was an Indian. We don't know what kind," I say.

Amy says, "Well, no I'm not rich. My people are from St. Mary Parish and are mostly fishermen. We're poor, like everybody else. They haven't recognized us as a tribe," she says and continues to shake the rain stick.

Amy says, "I like learning about different tribes just like you like learning about Rastafarians and Africans. I had to stop riding the bus because all of the black children were calling me racist because I protested one year about Black History Month. I wanted to know why we had Black History Month when we didn't have Native American Month. I mean right now, my people in Houma are facing so many problems, as much as you are, and no one is helping us. It's not that I wanted to stop your month. I wanted people to learn about us, too. Do you want to see my new book?" Amy asks.

"Sure," I say.

"This is a palm reading book. I can read palms now. Let me read your palm." Amy takes my hand. "You have the mystic cross of David which means that you are psychic. You will have two children, two boys. That's all I can do, now. I'm still learning," Amy says.

"If Maymay knew that you were reading my palm, she would ask me to get a switch. She always told me that she doesn't want me dabbling in witchcraft," I say.

"Well, your mama knows how to stop bleeding and cure ringworm. Everybody in the trailer park knows it, and they come to her for help. She helped to heal my sister and brother many times. People in Sunset are not like everywhere else. There are a lot of healers here. My grandfather was a healer. It's part of our culture," Amy says, and she shakes the rainmaker.

I call Vashan collect.

"Hi, I am so happy to hear from you. I miss you so much. I know that I am in love with you," Vashan says. He waits for me to say that I am in love with him.

"I am going to pick you up this Saturday. We will spend the whole day together. I want you to meet my parents and my friends," Vashan says.

"That would be great," I say.

I give him my address. I thank Amy for letting me use her phone and walk back home. The sky is turning dark now. I stop and stare deeply into the sky. I can hear the distant thunder. There is no rain. I think back to the picture of the Indian woman on Amy's living room wall. She has dark and wrinkled skin with high cheekbones. Her hair is adorned with a bandana, beads, and feathers. I imagine her chanting as she shakes the rain stick. Now, I listen to the thunder with no rain in the sky.

I stop and listen, just as I do with Maymay. There is one long ominous roll of thunder in the sky. I say, "My mother is going to leave me again."

Chapter 28

A Treasure Hidden in the Fields

Celeste

"'Again, the kingdom of heaven is like unto treasure hid in a field; the which when a man hath found, he hideth, and for joy thereof goeth and selleth all that he hath, and buyeth that field.' That's the King James version of Matthew 13:44." I tell Mr. Raymond. "You asked me if I was a treasure or if I was looking for a treasure in these fields? I am a treasure hidden in the fields."

I have to look up to Mr. Raymond because he is so tall. His white hair shines in the light, and his blue eyes burn straight through me. He reaches in his pocket and pulls out a crisp $20 bill and a nickel, just as he promised. He places them in my hand and holds up his right hand to give me a high five.

I raise my hand but then stop. "You have the mystic cross of David on your hand. My friend Amy does palm reading. She tells me that that means you are psychic," I say. "I wasn't supposed to say that. You are a Christian man. Many Christians don't believe in sorcery," I finish the high five.

"You are right. I am a prophet and a Pieces, a water symbol. I don't dabble in sorcery, but I know that the wise men were led by a star. They looked to the heavens. I don't dabble in witchcraft, but our God made the stars, prophets, and my hand," Mr. Raymond says. "I look to the sky for signs. You are the only young person in my church who has ever won that bet," he says. "I guess you wondering what I'm doing here at your school today. I'm here to talk about abstinence. It seems your counselor says one too many girls are coming up pregnant. You take care."

Mr. Raymond's speech is moving, and his presence is so powerful. He talks about saving yourself and how boys talk about their sexual encounter with girls when they are together like they talk about the color of their shoes. He tells us to save ourselves for our husbands. Flossy won the right to sell to the men in the field. She says that she is happy that I read my Bible and was able to quote the scripture he was talking about. People around town bought so much from us that year that we could have bought a small field and the treasure.

Chapter 29

American Beauties

Celeste

"Didn't you forget something?" Flossy says.

"What?" I ask.

"Your birth control pill. Here!" Flossy says.

I take the pill and swallow. I swallow every day, even though I am not having sex.

"So, you're going out with some rich foreigner. Me and your mama don't care, as long as you take your pills, and I watch your periods. I got your period on the calendar there in that kitchen. Your ovulation days are marked in red X's. You can't go out on dates on those days. You and Vashan young. Stuff stay in your body longer. Remember that. Open your mouth and lift your tongue," Flossy says. She examines my mouth and shoots me a mean look.

I like Flossy, even though she is mean and spiteful at times. I feel safe with her. She styled my hair like the lady in the magazine again. She has gotten so much better at it that she has been able to clip a pearl barrette in it. My mama has been buying clothes for me at the boutique, even though I've been getting Flossy to return most of them and invest in the business. I did keep a cotton flower sundress.

We sit on the red velvet sofa and wait for Vashan.

"Just because you have the pill doesn't mean you have to do nothing. You don't have to have sex just 'cause you on the pill. I want you to think about your grandmamma, T-Red, and Bumblebee all back there in Belle Place. I want you to think about your mama's reputation. She takes it with her wherever she goes. Think about it when that little boy feeling on your tiddies and trying to feel the wetness 'tween your legs," Flossy says.

Usually Flossy doesn't make me feel uncomfortable even when she walks around with her naked, dark man body, but I feel so uncomfortable with her now. I want my mama to be here with me. I want her to feel my stomach and make me laugh about butterflies and about being in love. Flossy is making me anxious, nervous, and regretful about being in love, and it's not a good feeling.

Soon, Vashan is there. He looks striking and handsome with his dreadlocks. He knocks, even though he is looking at my wide, bright eyes through the screen door.

He hands me the whitest box with a dozen roses. I've seen a lot of wild flowers and lilies, but never roses so pretty and red—so perfect.

"They are American Beauties. They are all fresh, except for one," Vashan says.

"This one is silk. I want you to have something to remember our first date when you are old and gray and married to me," he says.

I smell the roses. They smell so much better than the rose perfume that Maymay has. I lose track of time smelling the moist, soft roses. When I open my eyes, Flossy is standing at the aluminum screen door staring sternly at me.

Vashan gently puts his hands around my waist to help me down the steps. He opens my car door. He has placed rose petals on my seat and there is a book with handwritten poetry. He hands it to me. "These are some of my favorite love poems. I want you to read them when I am not here with you. Read them in the bathtub when you are taking a bubble bath," Vashan says.

"Where are we going?" I ask. Vashan is wearing Ray-Ban glasses. The wind is blowing through my curls in the convertible. He shifts the gear.

"I thought that we could go to my school festival. I then want you to meet my parents," Vashan says.

When we arrive at the festival, I meet his friends.

"Who is this, Vashan?" a white girl with blond hair asks. "She's pretty; where did you find her?"

"Her name is Celeste, and she is from Belle Place. I met her at the speech and debate competition."

"Oh, smart *and* cute. I excuse your rudeness, Vashan," the girl says. She turns to me. "My name is Samantha. I am in the gifted program with Vashan, and we live in the same subdivision. Vashan's dad is one of the best surgeons in Lafayette as well as the country. His mother is a gynecologist. They are like the Huckstables on steroids," Samantha laughs at her own joke.

"Vashan is a Rastafarian. Do you know what that is?" Samantha asks.

"Yes, I do, but I don't really feel like talking about it right now. I haven't seen Vashan in ages, and our time is precious together," I say.

Vashan says, "You are so right, Celeste. Let's get out of here."

Vashan drives me to his home.

The neighborhood has huge houses that are about five times the size of Maymay's house.

"I hope that your parents will like me," I say.

Vashan lives in a two-story brick house with matching his and hers Cadillacs.

We enter through the garage and then the kitchen. There is a woman with dreadlocks that looks like Vashan. She is beautiful with dark brown, shiny eyes that turn me into stone. I can barely move. His father is reading the newspaper. He seems so much friendlier than his mother.

"Hello. Vashan has a lot of good things to say about you. He said he couldn't call you because you didn't have a phone. My name is Dr. Matthew Smith," he says. His feet are propped up on his La-Z-Boy chair. He puts the footrest down, as well as his newspaper.

I think about my grandmother Maymay and what she said about rich people not understanding our poverty.

"I'm glad to meet you. This is my wife, Dr. Susan Smith. Why don't we have something to eat? We've been waiting for you," Dr. Matthew says.

I enter a grand dining room. There is a huge crystal chandelier that hangs above the silver, gold, and crystal glasses below. The table has been set, and all of the silverware and beautiful china is so overwhelming for me. I feel intimidated by the silverware and the maid who looks at me sternly as if I am using all of silverware and china incorrectly.

"Vashan tells me that you have researched Jamaica and the Rastafarians. Not all Rastafarians wear dreads. I'm sure you know. Vashan says you were surprised when you found out that Jamaica has cane fields," Dr. Smith says.

"I found out about the cane fields by reading some of the folk songs. You have really nice folk songs. Many of them tell sad stories. It's kind of like our zydeco and Cajun music. Both of them have beautiful dialect," I say.

Dr. Susan raises her brow. I guess she can't believe that I know such a word as dialect.

I can't enjoy the salmon because I am worried that I will eat incorrectly or spill something on my clothes. I place my hands in my lap. I remember Bumblebee telling me not to put my elbows on the table.

Dr. Susan tells me, "Why did you move to Sunset? Why are your other sisters and brothers still in Belle Place?" She stresses the word Belle Place. She tries to say it in her best French with a Jamaican accent.

This woman makes me feel uneasy. She has been looking at me the whole time, sternly and silently. She hasn't smiled yet. I know that she thinks that I am not good enough for Vashan. Dr. Susan does not wait for an answer to the first question, "Where is your daddy?"

The last question stabs me in the chest. I think about the red Xs on Flossy's Union National Insurance calendar with a picture of a field of purple wildflowers. I think about the old Creole house with the doorbell on the bedroom door and the Eagle's singing "Welcome to the Hotel California."

After a long pause pregnant with thoughts, images, and sounds of silverware, I say, "My grandmother said that I had too much passion for life. She wanted to see my hair loose. She wanted to see me leave Belle Place because my mother has the worst reputation in that... excuse me...I am going to say it just as she said it...'dead ass town,'" I grin as I think about Maymay and the expression.

"She said that she didn't want to see me depressed like my uncle who ended up killing himself in California when he was fired by the army. I think they call it A-Wall. He had to come back home to Belle Place, but he didn't want to. She wanted me to be happy. She wanted me to be free from ridicule," I say. I now feel sad, and I know that I probably look sad.

I look down at the immaculate white china place setting with bright red roses and nothing else. This place setting costs more than my Dollar General clothes. It is worth more than the five dollars that Mom Dot gave me to kill that mama cat. I could have a thousand times more if I could get Vashan to like me, but I will not let that bitch talk to me the way she is.

I look at Dr. Susan Smith straight in her cold, beautiful brown eyes. I am really falling in love with Vashan, but I am not going to put on a show for her.

"I don't know who my daddy is. My mother never told me. She says she doesn't really know. She slept with a lot of men in Belle Place. They call her the whore of Belle Place, and I know it's true because I've seen her kissing married men." I speak as politely as the words will allow me to. I place the white cloth napkin on the expensive china to show that I do not plan on eating her salmon. I wait for the Nubian goddess to tell Vashan to take me back home to the trailer park where I belong.

"You do indeed have a lot of passion. Never let it go. Passion will get you far. It got me out of the sugar cane fields of Jamaica into this grand house. It will get you where you need to be. Passion for life is a good thing," Dr. Matthew says. He points at me with his shiny fork, and places his own napkin on his plate as well.

"It was a wonderful thing your grandmother did. She let you go somewhere where you could enjoy your life and never be reminded of the sins of your mother. She must really love you. Vashan, this is a nice young lady. I like her."

He gets up, picks up his guitar and returns to his La-Z-Boy. "Vashan, since Celeste has researched my country and likes our songs, I am going to sing her an old Jamaican folk song. Then, I want the two of you to enjoy the rest of your precious night together. I want you to be a gentleman and take her home by her curfew. He sings to me:

Evening Time
Come Miss Celeste
Tek de banra off you head my dear,
Evening breeze a blow
Come dis way Miss Celeste.
Help down yah.
Afta you no beas' a burd'n mah
Ress yuh self at ease,
Feel di evenin' breeze.
Evenin' time,
Work is over now is evenin' time,
Wih deh walk pon mountain,
Deh walk pan mountain,
Deh walk pan mountainside.
Meck we cook wih bickle pan dih way,
Meck wih eat an sing,
Dance an play ring ding
Pan dih mountainside.
Ketch up dih fire Ma'hta
Pass me dih gungo peas,
Rub up dih flour Sarah - Lawd!
Feel di evenin' breeze

Dr. Susan escorts us to the door, while Dr. Matthew continues to sing. She says, "You people are still young. Enjoy yourselves. Don't take life too seriously, Celeste. Your thinking is too sophisticated for a young girl. Have some fun." She kisses both of us.

Vashan takes me to the football field at his school. No one is there. Everyone is at the festival. He places a blanket on the hood of his car, where we sit much like the day we first met.

Vashan is wearing Girbaud jeans and a football jersey. He smells like the expensive cologne in expensive magazines. I want to cuddle next to his strong bicep and just smell him and fall asleep.

"I didn't know that you played football. I thought that you were a nerd like me," I say.

He says, "I've made a lot of touchdowns on this field." He grabs me and places me on his lap. I want to say no, but I just want to smell him under the perfect starlit sky.

He places his warm dark hands over my breasts. My mama told me that I could relax because I was on the pill, but I am so uncomfortable. I say, "You have something in your pocket. It's hurting me. Take it out."

"I really wish that I could, but I can't. It's me." He wets his lips and kisses me and now I am paralyzed. He squeezes my breasts and begins to bite them with his strong, white teeth. He covers me in passion marks, and I can't move. I love the way his kisses feel, even the ones that hurt. I kiss him back. I am burning with desire. He reaches for my panties.

"Please don't go any further than this. Please!"

All of a sudden, he stops. He looks at me and says, "I want you to be my wife one day. You may not believe me, but I do love you. That's why I didn't tell you that I am a football player. I didn't want you to think that I am so dumb jock who just wants to have sex with you." He is now kissing me softly everywhere.

"One thing you have to know is that I am very possessive. I have a lot of uncles who would kill their wives for infidelity. I don't think that I could kill you, but I don't want you with no one else but me. I would do anything to make you only mine," Vashan says. He now kisses me on the face.

"Take me home. Now, please."

When I get home, Flossy says, "Make sure you take a hot bath before you get in my bed." I fill the tub all the way to the top. I take a bleach bath.

Dr. Matthew is probably singing a song to his beautiful Nubian wife. Black is calling Tut to come and get her medicine

I look in the full body mirror, and I don't recognize myself. My breasts are red and hurt, my neck and my face is bright read with one big passion mark. I plug in the curling iron. I know that if I burn myself, it will heal, but I will have a scar. I think of African tribes that Mrs. January told me about. The husband and wife mark themselves for each other. The only thing is Vashan will never mark me for him.

I burn my face. I feel like the field worker working with T-Man. I don't feel the flesh frying like bacon. I don't scream, and I don't cry. The next day I return the books about the Rastafarians and Jamaica.

"What happened to your face," the librarian asks.

"I burned it," I say.

No one owns me. I burn the roses and the poetry book that Vashan leaves by the steps. I think that Maymay is right. He is just a rich kid who thinks he owns me like he owns that white china plate with the roses. He just wants to mark me and use me. I don't want to be weak minded like my mama. I don't want to be marked for life like my mama. I don't want to be known as someone's whore. I want someone to love me and want me, and someday marry me. I want my children to know their daddy. I don't want to have illegitimate children like me. I can still smell his cologne on the black book. I toss the red roses first and the black book last. The fire consumes everything. Only the ashes are left the next day.

Chapter 30

Family Traditions

Celeste

Grinding is over. It is Christmas time. Tut and Flossy's business is doing very well in the trailer park. Now Flossy is selling peppermint baskets for the holidays. I sold several of them at my school. Everything seems to be looking up for my mama.

Mama hasn't seen her other children in a long time, and Maymay, T-Red, and the children think that it will be a good idea for her to come and visit them over in Belle Place.

"Mama's here," I hear my sisters yell. They run out of the house one by one to greet us. Maymay is making her famous pink cake for Christmas and stuffing her turkey with garlic and cayenne pepper. Mama and me walk in the living room. Our hair, makeup, and clothes all look great and everyone compliments us.

"I'm so glad to see y'all. I'm so glad. Everybody gonna be so proud...so proud of me," Mama says gleefully. Black drops two suitcases on the porch. He sits on the porch swing waiting for instructions from T-Red who walks from behind the yard where he was slopping his hogs.

He says, "Hey Black, what y'all say? I hear ya old girl doing good over yonder. Celeste doing good, too, in school. She mailed a copy of her report card to Maymay. Tut making money and keeping up the house. They say she not cutting up with them mens. I'm so proud. You proved me wrong Negro—proved me dead wrong. I guess you can make a ho a housewife." He elbows Black in the gut.

T-Red walks in the house and sees Mama smiling. He says, "Hey girl, I'm proud of you. I hear you doing good."

"I heard you on the porch. It's true. I'm doing great. I have a friend, something I never had here. We have a car and we are going to open our own Soul Food kitchen. We gonna be the talk of the town. The people here in Belle Place won't be able to talk about me no more. They gonna see what it is to make something out of yourself. I am doing better than most of them. Most of them just married, getting fat, and having babies. They don't know what it's to have they own business like me. I'm a business woman," Mama yells as she prances around in her fancy clothes. She is so proud and happy; she has finally proved everyone wrong.

Bumblebee says, "I even hear you and Celeste going to church out there. They say you going to the Catholic Church."

"Yeah, they let me take communion and everything. I pay my tithes with the money I make selling in the trailer and in town. Flossy gives me all of my receipts, and she lets me know how much I have to pay. She says we got to be honest about it or else we gon' be cursed," Mama says. "I just want to spend time with my children now. I brought some presents for them." Mama takes all of her children into the big middle bedroom. She gives them each a brand new present.

"I never had a present wrapped before. I don't know how to unwrap it," Tiny says as she hands the gift to me. I unwrap the present. Mama bought everyone a Sunday dress from a fancy department store. The girls are happy, and they rush out to try the dresses on.

Maymay walks in the room smiling and looking at Mama. She is holding her pipe and searching for her tobacco. "You two didn't make us shame yonder. Thank you so much. I am so proud of the two of you. We never had to go and fetch you hind nothing stupid. Now you back for the holidays." Maymay smiles. "And Celeste, I talked to Flossy. She told me how you let that foreigner go. I told you he thought he owned you. I'm glad you found out for yourself. He's still writing letters for you here. He say how he sorry and he want you to forgive him. He said his mama likes the way you stood up to her and how you didn't care what she thought about you. I am glad you didn't mess up your face with that curling iron." Maymay looks at me and touches her own face.

"His daddy says he'll never find anyone like you again. He said you a good country woman who woulda cooked for his son every day. You can read the letters. Tiny read them to me. He said that girl Amy always saying that she don't even know you. He some mad." Maymay stops and looks at me for a moment. She seems very happy that Vashan and I are no longer writing each other. I guess Maymay convinced me that someone like him wouldn't really want someone like me.

Why would he want to marry me? I think he said all of that because he wants to use me. The whole thing just seems too good to be true. A part of me wants to read the letters, but every time I think about my mama and all of the men who never wanted to claim my sisters and me, I just feel I can't trust someone like Vashan.

Maymay says, "You know we never had too much for Christmas, but we always had family a turkey roast, fixings, and ma pink cake." She smiles and wipes a tear from her face.

Maymay says, "T-Man always looked forward to that pink cake. Every Christmas he would say, 'Maymay go cut me a piece of that lop-sided pink cake.'" Maymay looks outside of the door long and hard as if she is searching for someone or something in those barren fields. "Yeah, the holidays not like they used to be. All the fun people gone." She places her pipe in her mouth and tries to savor its aroma.

Mama says, "Thank you for believing in me, Maymay, and giving me a chance. Thank you." She smiles at Maymay. "I want to tell all of y'all while you all are here. I'm going to have another baby. I'm four months pregnant. I'm going to take care of this one as much as I can all by myself. Don't worry, because I got Flossy there in Sunset to help me. She says she never had a baby in the family a long time, and she gonna help me raise it like it is her own.

"Black knows about it, and he looks forward to having another baby. He misses his children. He says that the house is not the same without children. He knows I am fertile as a rabbit, and it would be no time for me to bring him a baby. He stopped giving me my birth control medicine. He so excited. We found some stuff at the garage sale for the baby," Mama says. Her eyes are filled with glee.

"His ex-wife is all mad now and jealous that he is going on with his life. She wants him back. She crazy if she thinks he got to wait for her to make her mind up. When Flossy and I get our business together, I'm going to send money back here regular. You need to keep the money, Maymay. Stop mailing it back to me," Mama says.

Maymay says, "No sense in you giving these children empty promises. You with your scattered brain will have them looking through the window waiting. Go on with yo' life, Tut. We got things over ya. Worry about that nice looking black man in Sunset." She winks at Mama.

Maymay continues, "Well, you grown. I know you know how to take care of babies, but we don't have it hard like we used to. We've been getting child support for the twins. We just trying to find the father for Tiny and Celeste, and then we'll be fine as far as money goes. T-Red found the daddies of them two by asking around the fields and the car savage yard. They had him tested. You know people talk around Belle Place. They're helpful too.

"They know how hard it is for me, T-Red, and Bumblebee to raise all of these bad ass chillen with no money. Them chillen need stuff all the time for school. They want to dress and have the stuff like everybody else. Food stamps only go so far. You brought those sorry ass little presents, but we already bought them just what they wanted with they child support checks. They not wrapped pretty, but they got what they wanted. Bumblebee and T-Red been helping me good back ya. They even let them wear everything before Christmas, but they still got what they wanted and needed," Maymay says as she sits on the sofa.

Everyone knows she feels like a fish out of water on the sofa. Her rocking chair is not in its usual spot because T-Red is going to put some fancy carpet over the floor underneath her rocking chair. He is also getting the rocker reupholstered. She thinks that T-Red should just strip the linoleum and leave the cypress wood, but everyone wants what's new. Maymay begins to rock softly as she continues all of what she thought is wonderful news.

"T-Red really just wants you to 'fess up and give the names of them other two men so them girls can have a decent life like his children. T-Red got me a phone. When his income tax and bonus come, he gon' get me a window unit. I don't have a 220 plug, so he got to get a fella who gon' rewire the living room so I can have good air. I'll be able to cook more better and fry chicken like I used to. All you got to do is tell us the name of them other two men," Maymay says.

She turns and yells, "Tiny go see where Kojo done hide my tobacco so I can smoke ma pipe. Kojo's always messing with ma stuff. I should go hide that sock of his," Maymay says as she picks up speed rocking in her imaginary rocking chair.

Mama has an anxious look on her face. She begins to wring her hands. She walks out of the room. T-Red and Black are still talking on the porch. T-Red sits on the porch swing next to Black admiring his newfound friend. He praises Black for performing a miracle. Black says, "Well, I better go. What time you want me to pick you up after New Years?" he asks Mama, who is staring.

T-Red yells, "Tut—that man talking to you. You better tell him something. I'm not riding over there. I'm going to be enjoying the holiday with my old woman."

Tut continues to stare and says softly, "Whenever you pick me up is fine."

Black gets into the Buick, makes a U-turn in the yard, and accelerates quickly down the gravel road.

T-Red looks at Tut and jokingly comments, "*Mais,* look at how your old brown peeling out of here fast. I know you giving that man hell in Sunset. He look like he ready to get rid of you. I know how you carry on something terrible here. I can only imagine what's going on yonder."

Mama says, "He knows I am happy to see my family. I'm the one who wanted to bring in the year with everyone. He likes me. He just thinks that all of us are very weird."

T-Red says, "Well, Tut, if you so good how come you don't call your own children now that mama got her own phone now. You hollering about how you a businesswoman and you can't even make a business call to them children. When we call Celeste at Flossy's house now that she got a phone, Flossy say you barely talk to your own daughter. Celeste don't even go to your house. She just go to the library and read books with Flossy. Well, let me tell you something, gal. Those children know about you, and they watch out for each other. They not studying about you. They try to act like they is 'cause Maymay want them to know they mama, but them girls doing good now with me and Bumblebee help."

T-Red says, "Black tells me you pregnant. Don't worry about these children. They happy ya. We doing good by them. Just take care of the one over yonder in your belly. I hear Flossy is a good friend. That's something you never had in Belle Place."

Tut shouts, "She is my best friend. Do you understand?"

T-Red says, "Damn, I guess I do" T-Red brushes off his cowboy boots. T-Red is dressed up. He even has expensive cologne on, not like the cheap one Black wears. He has alligator boots, a starched white dress shirt, blue jeans, and a heavy silver cowboy belt.

He and Bumblebee are going to go out to a New Year's Eve ball at some hole in the wall club with no name in Cecilia where they will bring their own food and swing out and zydeco.

Bumblebee plans to share her table with her mother and her aunts. Cooking the night before, she has a honey ham, black eyes peas with greasy pig tails, cabbage, buttered corn bread, and better than sex cake.

Mama says, "I hear you telling Black that you are going out to a ball. I thought that Bumblebee doesn't go out,"

T-Red says, "Bumblebee do what she want when she wants to," T-Red says with a smirk. "She can be holy roly, or she can be roly poly, if you know what I mean. Hell, you have kids, you know what I mean. Bumblebee wants to go swing out tonight. They gonna have zydeco and everything there tonight. I'm going to dance and show that girl a good time. She says that we can enjoy the sins of the flesh 'cause we married. There is nothing unlawful she can do to me," T-Red laughs and slaps Mama on the back.

Bumblebee parks her new car. She has a late model Buick Riviera much like Black's. She lets the automatic window down and shouts, "Hey, Tut and Celeste, come on in. Let's go take a ride."

Mama and me get in. Bumblebee says, "Take off your shoes before you get in my car." We take off our shoes and get in.

"This is a nice car," Mama tells Bumblebee.

Bumblebee says, "I know what you thinking. We got this car to outdo y'all. We got this car because T-Red is all the time tracking mud in his car. I got tired of it, so I got my own car. I can carry the girls and Maymay in this car. We have more room than in the Nova. Besides, Maymay liked that car that Black has. She wanted one, too. Did T-Red tell you that we are going after them mens you messed with?"

"Yeah, he told me." Mama says. Well, I know one of them works at Leblanc store. Why don't you go talk to him and see if he'll agree to something so we don't have to take him to court. I need to go fix some more food for the ball. I don't have enough. We have to bring sandwiches and deviled eggs."

When we arrive at Leblanc's, Bumblebee disappears into the aisles to leave us to fend off the stares and mean looks.

"Tut. Tut...Is that you Tut?" Papoo calls from the crackling and boudin counter. Papoo was always Mama's off and on friend in high school.

"I didn't recognize you, Tut. Your hair all done up, you got on your rabbit fur jacket and knee boots. You look like one of them white girls in *Glamour* magazine. Go head, Tut! You look bad, and I do mean good. I took you for a rich white woman until I heard you talking to Bumblebee," Papoo says. She looks at Mama from head to toe and then gives her a high five. She looks at me and tells me hello, too.

"You know what they say about the Mulattos you can't tell that they white or black until they open they mouth. Once they open they mouth, that's it," Mama says as she smiles at Papoo.

"Yeah, Tut, when T-Red comes here to buy his crackling, he always bragging about you. I see what he bragging about. You look like a model. You look some good. Well, you always look good, but you especially look good, now. Them people in Belle Place gon' be shocked to see you, girl," Papoo says as she bags cracking behind the counter.

Papoo is being so nice to her when only about a year or so ago she beat her merciless on the side of Leblanc's Grocery store.

"How are you and Bo doing?" Mama asks.

"Well, Bo still messing with women behind my back. I let him go, Tut—let him go," Papoo says as she stares past the isles. Mama looks at her disbelievingly because she knows that Papoo has been breaking up with Bo and getting back with him again for four years. The next time she will talk to her, they will probably be married.

"I let him go. I should've stayed friends with you. I am the only friend you had in Belle Place. Maybe you would've been able to stay yonder with your people in the sugar cane fields if I would a kept up with ya. I used to help Maymay keep you in line." Papoo looks at Bumblebee who has a basket that is piled high with food.

"Ya remember how we would knock on the classroom doors and run? Boy they could never catch us. We were so fast. I miss those days." Papoo says, and she and Mama smile as they think about Mrs. Washington trying to catch them as they would hide behind the curtains of the stage.

Mama whispers, "Yeah, I remember those days."

"I used to keep you out of trouble. I would tell people not to fight you. You never knew how to fight, but you were always picking fights. You were something, girl," Papoo says and smiles at Mama.

Mama tells Papoo about her new life in her quick, childlike way, "I have a friend over there in Sunset. We gonna open a business. It's not gonna be big like Leblanc's. Leblanc's has a bakery, a butcher, boudin and crackling counter, and a plate lunch counter. We won't have all of this, but it's gonna be nice. We've been looking at aluminum buildings. It will be a hole in the wall to start off. Then we gonna expand like we been expanding our business. We started with a grocery cart. Now we have a car," Mama says. Mama comes alive with her story.

"That sounds nice. I would like to go there. Whenever I leave Belle Place, which is not often, I'll look it up. What y'all gonna call it?" Papoo asks disbelievingly.

Mama's eyes are wild and wet with excitement. She shrieks, "Tut and Flossy's."

"Cute," says Papoo as she wipes the white counter, "really cute."

"Yeah, it has a soul food ring to it like those restaurants in the big city," Mama says.

Babette is walking through the aisle next to where Papoo and Tut stand. She glances at Mama without saying anything. Mama wants to make sure that she sees her, so she waves hello and tries to get her attention. Babette looks at her and rolls her eyes. Refusing to acknowledge her, she dodges eye contact from my mama.

Babette is the wife of the father of the twins. He is now, thanks to T-Red and Bumblebee, paying child support for the two kids. Babette tells Papoo, who stands in amazement behind the counter, "Give me eight links of boudin and $5 worth of crackling." Papoo and I can both feel the hateful look that Babette has on her face and the nervous fear that my mama has on her face. Papoo gets busy getting her order ready with a smug grin and wide eyes. We both feel like an argument is going to happen any minute now.

Papoo avoids eye contact with both Babette and my mother.

Tut wants Babette to see her in her nice store-bought and not garage sale clothes. Mama wants her to see her now, and not the whore of Belle Place, "Hey Babette how you doing?"

Babette turns slowly in Mama's direction. Babette looks up and down at Mama and says slowly and carefully, "Listen bitch, just cause you can put a little clothes on your trifling ass and wash the funk off you don't mean you can stride in this store and stand in front of me and expect I'll listen or react to every look and word you tell me."

My mama looks confused. Her mouth is slightly open, and she stares into Babette's eyes. She just lets her tell her how much she really hates her.

"No one gives a damn about you or your little shit you got going on in the country over there in Sunset. You're trying to come after me and Butch check. Your no-good family trying to come after all kind of people. They're trying to turn Belle Place over and upside down to find out all the men you done fucked. You better watch it, girl. A lot of people say they gonna mess you up if they find you, and I may just tell them I found you trying to be recognized, trying to return fucking curtsies to me. Just 'cause you got a rabbit fur jacket on and a little outfit. That don't mean nothing. Get a rabbit's foot bitch. You gonna need it if you plan on spending any time in this a here town." Babette points to the rabbit foot on her key chain.

"People work too hard around here for you to go meddling in they pocket books. If I wasn't a Christian woman, I would beat you right here and now, but I still got a good reputation that I can live out in my town. I don't have to run nowhere to run away from what I done out ya. You always going be trash in this town with your rabbit fur and your little fit. You are trash. Do you need me to spell it fa ya, heifer? Well, here it go T-R-A-S-H—trash." Babette counts on her five fingers to spell out each letter. She then makes a fist and puts it in Mama's face.

She now turns her attention to Papoo and looks at her up and down after fixing the barrette in her little girl's hair. "Papoo, watch who you talk to is all I'm saying. You don't want her dragging you down, either. You know what they say misery loves company. You're the only one in this town who tried to show her some kindness, and look how she tried to go after Bo. Watch yourself girl. You know they mess with that hoodoo too. Watch yourself."

With that, she takes her crackling and boudin places them in the basket and strolls off with her full basket of neatly placed groceries. A long ponytail whirls behind the top of her huge behind as she walks away looking at the sale paper and putting items in her already loaded basket.

Papoo says, "Don't pay her no mind. She just bitter. This town is full of big, black, bitter women. I would be that way too if I didn't take life as seriously as they do. Her old man calmed down since they threatened to put him in the pen behind those two children. He is not cutting up on her, and he knows he needs to hold a job. Just be careful around here." She gives Mama a look of pity and drifts off into the aisles to continue her morning duties. Mama walks off and looks at Papoo one more time. Papoo winks at Mama and gives her the peace sign.

Mama says, "Let's find Bumblebee. I want to go back home." She doesn't want anyone from Belle Place reminding her of who she is or where she comes from. Her life is so different in Sunset.

She walks through the aisles and calls Bumblebee's name softly. She tells me, "Maybe she's back at the car. Let's go back to the car." On our way out, we see Bumblebee grabbing a gallon of milk.

Bumblebee always takes her time. She spends hours shopping. You can never rush her.

Mama says, "Bumblebee can we have the keys to the car so I can go sit in it. I don't want to be in this store. People are being mean to me." Mama shifts her feet from left to right and looks at the floor. She is trying to avoid the stares.

"Hell no," shouts Bumblebee. "I don't want you snooping around in my car. I brought you here so you can go and talk to that dude in the meat department. You need to see if he gon' go take the test before T-Red go to the court house next week and get him summoned," Bumblebee says.

Tut says, "I can't do that."

Bumblebee says, "Wait, come on here, I'll come with ya. I always got to do every damn thing for this family. Celeste, the dude in the meat department might be your daddy. I want to look at y'all together to see if you two look alike."

Bumblebee marches over through the aisles until she makes it to the meat market. She stops when she sees the manager of the meat market, a tall goofy looking white man. Bumblebee says, "Is Walter Lee Batiste working today?"

The manager says, "Yes, ma'am," with a friendly smile.

"Can you get him for me please?"

"Sure." He walks into the meat cutting room and calls for him. "Walter Lee—Mrs. Bumblebee wants to talk to you."

Bumblebee looks at Mama. "You see how them people know me here. I got pull. Hear how he says 'Mrs. Bumblebee want to see you?' They know I don't play around here. I be turning this whole store out when they don't give me good service." A mean-looking, tall black man comes to the meat counter. It is Walter Lee, one of Mama's old lovers that might be my daddy. He has a look of disgust and tries to go back to the cutting room.

Walter Lee says, "Ah no, man. It's you again. I tell you to stop harassing me on my job. I'm going to put a restraining order on you if you don't stop harassing me," he says.

I can tell that he is trying to use his intelligent voice and his big words. His voice sounds pretentious. I can't imagine this man being my father. He is tall like me, but I don't think I look like him much. I look like my mother, so I am trying to look at his hands or ears or something else on his body that is similar to my body.

"And me and Maymay gonna put child support on you if you don't take care of this kid." She points at me like I am a thing.

He doesn't even look at me. He looks in Mama's direction. Mama is facing the opposite direction. She will not look at him. She just stares at her boots the whole time. All he sees is my mama's pretty sandy brown hair, a rabbit fur coat, and long legs in straight leg jeans.

Ignoring Bumblebee's long, drawn-out speech about money, children, and the law, he continues to look at my mama. Bumblebee continues to hurl insults. He asks the long hair, "May I help you, miss."

Slowly, Mama turns around. She lifts her head. At first he doesn't recognize her, but as she moves her hand away from her face, he whispers, "Tut."

Mama says, "Just know I never asked nobody for nothing. Nobody ever helped us all these years. I don't want nothing now. Bumblebee and T-Red's pushing all of this. I'm just here visiting my family. I never knew it was going to be all of this mess. T-Red been asking around and people gave him your name. I'm just here visiting."

Bumblebee yells, "Bullshit. Tut, I'm not playing with you, *non*. I'm not going to help take care of all of them children if you don't make these niggers support they kids. That shows what a trifling mother you is. You don't give a damn about them kids. People don't have time doing for your kids with no money. You think you did something by bringing those little cheap raggedy Dollar General presents with that cold cup money you got. Nobody gon' take care of those kids with no money, Tut. Not Maymay, not Red, and for damn sure not Bumblebee."

Walter Lee looks at Mama. "Tut, please stop embarrassing me with these accusations. Tell your family I have nothing to do with making this child. Maybe I had a drink with you at The Red Wheel Barrow, but that is it. My wife knows I go there every now and then with the fellas to hang out after a long day of work," Walter Lee tells Mama. Neither of them can look each other face to face. Mama looks down at the floor, and Walter Lee looks just past her.

I know that through the many conversations that my mama has had with Maymay that she isn't sure of any of the fathers of the children, especially me and Tiny. I've always wanted to know who my father was, but I can't be sure that this man is my father at all.

"Walter, I tell my people I don't know the father of my children," Mama says as she lowers her head deep into her full bosom. She says it low, but loud enough for Bumblebee, Walter, and me to hear. "Everybody in this town knows my business. I slept with a lot of men. I don't know where to begin to look. It's like trying to find a needle in a haystack. I don't want to embarrass anyone. No one should have to suffer for all of my sorry mistakes. Not even you." Her spirits and her voice are going down with every word she says.

Bumblebee stands there in between the two of them. She begins to swing her arms and punch her fist in her open hand in a rhythmic motion. "All right, that's cool. I see where this is going. You trying to scare her." She points at his face with a long nail. "Your papers *will* be in the mail," Bumblebee says.

"You got you a little dirty coochie from Tut. You don't want to pay the price now. Next time use a rubber. You trying to talk all proud in front of these ya white folks. All the good black folks know you just as much trash as Tut for what you did to that poor woman that used to be your wife. You beat her like she was a piece of raw meat you cut up every day. I hope you rot in jail for not taking care of ya chillen. You gon' rot, you fake ass nigger. You gon' rot." She looks at the manager who is peeping at her from the back of his office.

"Y'all better know better than calling the law for me. Last time, I almost shut this store down when ya'll tried to call the cops on me. As much money as I spend up in ya, y'all better not call no police fa me. Don't make me start a boycott." Bumblebee screams as she walks away from Walter Lee.

She pays for her groceries and grabs Mama by her long hair and pushes her in front of her. She yells, "Get your skinny little ass in the car. I'm going to tell Red you made me shame in front of all these people. You lucky I don't fight no more cause I'm Christian. I should beat your ass in front of all of these people." Mama turns around to look at Bumblebee. She can't believe that she pulled her hair.

Chapter 31

Let's Go Walk in the Fields

Celeste

Living in a small town like Belle Place, there is nothing much to do to pass the lonely minutes that turn to abandoned hours and run into the deserted days. Mama sits on the sofa watching television. She is going to stay up and watch the Dick Clark special with Maymay and me. We like looking at how people in the big city so far from Belle Place enjoy the New Year in their pretty clothes and hats and horns. We watch the special every year together. We never miss it.

Every New Year's Day, the kids pop firecrackers outside in the big yard. T-Red goes to Black Cat Fireworks, a big tent in town, and buys the kids about fifty dollars of fireworks. He doesn't worry about their safety. He allows the kids to pop the fireworks at their own risk.

As soon as his car pulls up on the headland, the children yell, "Fire crackers!" and run behind his slowly moving car. Once he opens the door, the children wait for him to give the fireworks to Liver, who divvies them up. They wait until 10 o'clock and they begin to pop them one by one.

Suddenly, Maymay wakes up. "What's all that damn racket?" She grabs her pipe from the table next to her chair. She lights it. I washed her hair and scratched her dandruffs. Her long gray and black hair is brushed back in a braid like Amy wears. Maymay looks like an old Indian woman.

I washed all of the clothes because Maymay never wants to bring in the New Year with dirty clothes in the hamper. We would not bring dirty clothes into a New Year day. That is bad luck. Tomorrow we will eat black-eyed peas for luck and greens for money through the year.

One thing the family does on slow days is to take a walk in the fields. In the fields, we talk about the past, the present, and what life may hold in the future for our lives.

Mama says, "Celeste. Why don't you come with me and take a walk in the fields." Maymay is dozing off now as she slowly rocks back and forth. The children are popping firecrackers in the ditch and in bottles. Bumblebee and T-Red are practicing their swing out for the ball.

"Bon Ton Roulet" by Clifton Chenier is playing on the radio in the house. The house smells like holiday food. There is spicy stuffed turkey, savory pork roast, rice dressing, macaroni and cheese, and Maymay's pink lemon soda cake.

"Okay Mama, we can talk like we want to out in the fields." I put on my designer tan coat and slip on my new boots Bumblebee got me for Christmas. The ground is wet with cold ice. The sugar cane has been cut and burned. The burnt smell of sugar cane is so familiar, especially today. The cold air and the smell and sound of firecrackers as well as holiday foods puts everyone in a festive mood. The sky is dark and the clouds are low and cold. I never had a close relationship with Mama. Even the close time that we spent in her trailer was rare but precious to me.

Mama never tries to talk to me much. There are slight bursts of wind in the now darkening and peculiar sky. I can tell that my mama has something important to tell me.

Walking in the fields is always nice. These walks often help us search our souls. Today I feel I will dig deep. They say when you die, your life passes before you, and you see pictures of the past. That's what walking through the fields is like. You can talk about the past and the memories are like pictures that are in your mind. We talk about the memories and laugh just as we did back then when they happened. Mama and me begin our walk. I can tell that Mama has a lot to talk about.

Mama says, "I know that Diana Ross made those songs, but I did make some of them, too. I think that I get like Maymay when

I'm stressed out. That's what Flossy tells me. I'm not worried about the secret place. When I think about it, I get embarrassed. You can keep that box of stuff, though." I can tell that she has something important to tell me, but she doesn't want to get to it right away.

Mama says, "Flossy says that I lose my mind, sometimes. She read a medical book to me about the two personalities. If Black don't come and get me soon, I'm going to go crazy again with or without my medicine. Flossy says that I can go a few days without it. She doesn't like to see me sleepy anyway. Walking has been my way out with Flossy. It calms both of us. That's why I asked you to come with me. I don't know. I just miss home. I don't like coming here. I don't feel safe."

We talk about a lot of things. I tell Mama about how I won a national writing contest and now there is a certificate with her name at the school board in Sunset. I say, "I think I learned to write so well because I read the *Bible* so much. They say that the King James Version of the *Bible* is the best-written book in the world. I love to write Mama," I say.

Mama is proud that a Bastille can do something like that. "At least our name will go down for something good. I guess Maymay and T-Red will be biting their words and their tongue. One of Tut's daughters finally did something to make the family look good," Mama says.

I feel that she is actually listening to me. I continue, "I got to eat in a fancy restaurant. The principal took me. Flossy bought me a nice outfit and gave me fifty dollars, but I didn't need it because they paid for everything. The principal and the school board people were really impressed. I took a picture with the *Sunset News*."

We can hear the firecrackers popping in the distance. Then when we are about halfway through the fields, we look behind them and Maymay, the children, and Bumblebee are coming towards us. "It's always been that way. When one walks, they all want to walk. They all want to follow behind and see what we're talking about," Mama says.

We hold on to each other and laugh. Bumblebee is holding her baby on her big breast and Maymay's old legs are walking faster than anyone else.

"Bumblebee and T-Red are treating everyone really good from what they tell me in letters and here. They say that I am stupid for living with you because they've been getting whatever they want, and they don't have to work as hard. Bumblebee and T-Red are trying to get the money from our fathers to pay on a lot of our things we need. Bumblebee and T-Red say even though I am three years away from making eighteen, and I won't get child support anymore, I still need to know who my father is, and the extra money can help them. I don't care who he is. Bumblebee is sharing. She still doesn't let anyone fool with her house, but she really is good to the kids. They are going to buy Maymay an air conditioner," I say.

"I'm glad everything is working out," Mama says. "I need to tell you about your father. Everybody else is finding out about their fathers. Bumblebee and T-Red are digging up dirt, so you will find out about your father soon, especially if he is tested like the twin's father was. I want to tell you about yours. I think, although I am not 100 percent sure, it's Walter Lee Batiste just like Bumblebee and everybody else thinks. You met him at the store. You are tall like him. I'm not sure because I was raped. He and another man are the only two that went in me. The other two did other nasty stuff to me, but not sex in between my legs. If it would have been the other one, you would have been lighter because he is light like me."

Mama says, "He is that butcher you saw at Leblanc's. I never told y'all about your daddies because none of them ever wanted me. They just used me. I don't know why I let people use me. It's been hard living here. I just wanted nice things, and all of them sure knew how to lie to me. They would lie to me, and I would believe them. He was mean to me. He raped me the first time and said I was nothing but trash. I liked him 'cause he would always call me pretty girl. Don't ask me why I wanted a man who raped me. I guess that is why I am sick. I am not right in the head. He was married at the time, so I really didn't tell nobody and no body in a town like this would think that someone like me was raped. It was too much for me to handle. If you see him, promise me you will walk the other way,"

"I promise," I say.

Mama's eyes are wet and wild. She has fear. She wants to go back to the safety of her Kool-Aid packs and Flossy's warm velvety pillows on the floor. She wants to go back to Black's trailer with the engines in the house and Black's kind familiar smile. She likes being home, but she doesn't like the look that Walter Lee gave her in town. It reminds her of what she was and the hurt and pain she has felt in life.

I can't imagine someone like Walter Lee being my daddy. My mama had me for someone who raped her. I think that maybe this is why she could never get close to me. I know one thing. If Walter Lee raped my mama, I don't want to get close to him. I don't want him to recognize me as his daughter. This is all a little too much for me to take in at this time. I say, "Let's turn around. Maymay gonna kill herself trying to keep us with us."

We turn around, and in about twenty minutes, we are with the gang. Maymay continues her familiar ranting about the new neighbors. In a huge outburst, she begins pointing and gesturing.

Maymay says, "Tut, you see that trailer over there. *Mais,* that wasn't there before. Belle Place is growing. Every time they chop the cane, you see more and more new places. *Mais,* I'm going to start keeping my door locked now. They got mo' people back ya. Lord knows where they come from. You know the city folks not like the country folks." Maymay slows her pace now that she is walking with us. Bumblebee is passing her baby around. She is out of breath. She has on her warm-ups and roach killer shoes, as she calls them. They are flat, no-name tennis shoes. She wouldn't wear anything nice in the fields.

"I thought I'd come walk in the fields with y'all before I go out to the ball. I know I'm going to eat tonight. I might as well burn some calories. Don't worry, Tut, we gonna go after Walter Lee. He don't scare me and T-Red. He can beat up on them other women and scare them. Let him mess with me. I'll show him where to get off. I'm not the one. I'll walk his ass all the way to the jailhouse. We got into it so bad the other day, they had to kick me out of Leblanc's," Bumblebee says as she huffs and puffs along the trail.

As the house gets closer and closer, they talk and laugh about the good old days when Mama and me were living with them. Everyone seems so happy. It is like old times.

Mama calls Black when she gets home. She says, "I'm really ready to come home now. I don't want to be here no more. The town people are mad at me. My family done stir up a lot of mess."

Mama tells me that Black says he is going to bring us back to Sunset tomorrow.

Chapter 32

There is Blood in Tut's Secret Place

Tut

My life is getting harder to understand, and my memory is like a foggy cloud. I am talking to myself today and laughing as hard as I can about old jokes. I look at our family's old funeral pictures when T-Man died.

Maymay is so angry, and Celeste gives me a suspicious look. Celeste says, "This picture is not funny. We went through a lot of pain that day."

I laugh because we are all in matching black dresses. The women all wear matching black lace head rags that Maymay sewed herself while her husband was dying. We just look so organized. Bumblebee is the only one smiling. She look like she proud to be in our family. She always protects us. I laugh at the likeness. I laugh at our snobbish attitudes. I laugh at our strength. I wish I could explain it, but I can't. I think that maybe I am entertaining demons like Flossy say when I laugh all day long to myself about something no one thinks is funny. No one needs to know the reason.

I leave the stacks and stacks of photo albums that sit on the floor and I go to the restroom and look at myself. My hair look good with the brown and orange fur of my rabbit jacket. My jeans feel gritty and tight along all the curves of my body. My long leather boots hug the thick calves of my skinny legs like one of my crawling children holding on to my leg. The heels make my walk sexier than anything. My belly is hard, but I don't look pregnant, yet. I look a little chubby.

No one understand me but my secret place and my sugar cane secret room. I look out at the dark sky where the blue is mixed with browns. I see cars passing far away where the land meets someone else's sky. The cars look like little ants moving. Houses all alone in deserted fields hold people dreaming, like me. Most of my dreams are true. I still want a doublewide trailer. I still want Black to marry me. Black tells me he might if his wife don't act right. I hate the way he still calls her his wife. It seem like his wife is everything, and I am nothing. I only have country girl dreams, made in this field and lost in this field.

I am walking in high-heeled boots through a dirt road. I see our tree. I can't remember if it ever had leaves or what it is doing in the middle of a sugar cane field. Why did the farmer leave it planted here? I stop and look back at my children who are rummaging through the yard in search of old firecrackers. They are poking the bushes with their sticks. Every now and then I hear one go off.

They would probably ask me if they could join me if they wasn't having so much fun. I am happy that no one noticed me. Soon, I can no longer hear Maymay cussing the television set, the smell of tobacco, or popping firecrackers. I don't see T-Red and Bumblebee's rocking trailer from their wild sex games. Soon, they will go off into some dark corner and listen to their old songs and drink old wine while naked. It's almost night.

I sat on yellow, purple, and pink wildflowers in these fields at one time and wrote my songs. I looked at the sky and slept. I practiced the latest dance moves, so that no one could make fun of me. I came here to sit and look at my magazines.

I have one of Maymay's fresh sheets, straight off of the clothesline. I place it in between rows that once had sugar cane. I lay there and stare up at the now darkening sky. My body is warm. I feel swaddled in the earth like a baby. There is one row on either side of me. As I look up at the peaceful, setting sun I wonder who else is letting the earth coddle them to sleep. I fall asleep.

I feel terror. I open my eyes. Someone is on the row to the left of me, and looks into my eyes. I can't make out the dark face. I grab the sheet and wrap it around me. I forget that I am fully clothed. I don't recognize him.

I say, "I'll be leaving soon. I just wanted to take a rest in the field. I wanted to get away from my crazy house." Suddenly, the old beliefs of Maymay come back. I could be seeing a Black Fucker.

"It's me, Walter." His breath smells like cheap whisky.

He says, "I see you in town looking all cute and sexy. How come you never look like that for me? Your hair all done up and everything, looking like a white girl in the magazines."

"Taytay, who lives in Mrs. Canoe's old house called and told me that somebody was walking in the fields by your house," Walter Lee says. "She said it looked like a prostitute. We all knew it was you. I drove my daddy tractor to come meet you. You can't hide nothing in this town. I see you not meeting nobody. I thought I'd come and get me a little bit for old times' sake with the new and improved Tut." Walter Lee smiles at me and I am scared to death.

I say, "Look, I don't care about no child support. Just let me go. If you send the checks to Maymay, I'll pay you back. Just let me know which day. I don't want nothing. I just want to go back to Sunset."

The field looks like a dark room with only the smell of dirt reminding me that I am outside. Maymay probably has the TV blasted on the highest volume, since she is losing some of her hearing. If I try to scream, I know that no one will hear me.

Walter Lee says, "Oh, now since you been up there in Sunset you think you too good for me. You think I can't do you like that dude with that Buick." Walter Lee holds on to me and rocks me back and forth. He holds my body with one hand and takes my belt off with the other hand. "I got ya Buick right over ya," he whispers in my ear.

I don't want him touching me. He makes me think about everything bad in my past. Walter Lee has always made me have sex with him even when I didn't want to. He would lie and tell me that he is going to give me money and leave his wife for me. He even promised to stand in for Celeste's christening. Although, he never beat me like his wife, he is as evil as they come in Belle Place. I feel his evilness and terror now.

I don't know how, but I get away from him. I kick him in his dick with my heavy boots. I try to run as fast as I can. I can't hide in the plowed sugar cane field. It doesn't take someone like him long to get me. I scream as loud as I can.

He hops on his tractor and says, "I'm going to beat your ass, you high yeller bitch." He cranks up the tractor and comes after me. I know that I am running for my life so I have to run as fast as I can. I jump over rows it seems two at a time. I don't feel the pain of my body. I want to save my life, but I fall and sprain my ankle.

He presses the gas as hard as he can, and the tractor plows my body with the dirt. He is afraid to look back once he runs over me.

When he finally stops the tractor, he sits there for a moment in silence. He looks up to the sky and takes a deep breath. He lets it out. He puts his hands on his forehead. He knows that he will have to get down eventually and look at what he did to me.

After jumping off of the tractor like a savage cowboy at a trail ride, it finally hits him when he sees my dark, bloody body in the plowed up dirt. He doesn't believe that he killed me. I know that Walter Lee is stupid, but did he really think that he could fuck me after cutting my body up with a tractor? He still has the desire to fuck me, but I don't look as good as I did when he met me in the fields.

He takes the sheet and puts all of what's left of my body in it. He drives to a crawfish pond, not too far from the Teche Bayou, and throws the sheet and my body into the pond. He knows that they will never find the bits and pieces because the crawfish will eat my torn-up flesh. "They'll never find you now," he whispers as he looks at me going to the bottom of the pond.

Night passes, and everyone wonders where I am, "*Mais,* that's not like Tut to leave and not tell us where she's going. I'm going to call Sheriff Picard to see if he can find out where Tut went off to. Call Bumblebee and T-Red," Maymay says to Celeste.

Bumblebee and T-Red are there in a hurry. They go looking all over to try to find me, but they can't find me.

I am missing now for two days.

Sheriff Picard comes with his little pot belly to Maymay's house and says, "Y'all think where she can be? Think hard now. Think! We don't have a lot of time." Celeste sits there quietly crying.

"I think I know where I can find her," she says. She tells everybody how I would go to my secret place and maybe I am there in the fields. The sheriff rides with my daughter through the headlands.

Celeste says, "She always calls it her secret place. She never wanted me to tell anyone about it," When she spots the tree, she says, "It's near that tree, in that vicinity." Celeste can't bear to look. The sheriff goes with his deputy, and they find blood and guts in the field but no body. They know that I am dead.

They tell everyone to leave the area. The next day, a group of crime scene people come to gather evidence.

Bumblebee calls Black. "Tut done fell into some trouble. Those people been around here taking everything out of our yard and fields. They even took the chicken bones we threw out for the dogs. We don't know what happened to her."

T-Red is on the porch. He or anyone in the house rarely cries, but he wipes tears from his face. He is so upset over the news. "Me and Bumblebee should've mind our own business. She could've been here enjoying the last of the holidays with us. God knows where she is now," T-Red says.

T-Red gets in his Nova and goes to Leblanc's. He is going to talk to Walter Lee. He storms into the store and goes directly to the meat department. He asks the manager, "Where the hell is Walter Lee?"

"Walter Lee doesn't work here anymore. I'm sorry to hear about Theresa. We said a rosary for her. She was a nice girl. She was trying to get her life together and everything," the manager says.

T-Red visits the other men who were paying child support for my children. They all seem like they don't have anything to hide. Walter Lee knows that T-Red wouldn't go to his home. It would be an excuse for Walter Lee to shoot him. T-Red just lays low and waits for word in the street as to Walter Lee's whereabouts. T-Red would find him in the streets and deal with him.

He tells all of the regulars at the Red Wheel Barrow as they sip on their drinks, "When I find Walter Lee in the streets, I'm going to kick his ass. I don't care if he did it or not. I'm going to wear him out just for seeming suspicious and being gone all of a sudden. That is my only sister. I don't care that she had problems. I am supposed to protect her." Everybody knows T-Red around Belle Place. They know that he is a fair fighter and a good fighter. He carries his gun, but he always fights with his hands.

Maymay says, "I love Tut. I never told her that, but I always tell everybody I love all my children. We never talk about love. She just thought that I was all the time mad at her. I sure am proud of all the things she done yonder in Sunset. She had so much going for her. Now this."

Maymay tells everyone in the room as she rocks in her rocking chair, "We don't have a body. We can't wake her. I've been known to stay with the body overnight. That smart little girl, Celeste, says I am worse than an elephant. I mourn till the death long gone. We can't bury her. All we see is her blood yonder in them sugar cane stumps."

Maymay says, "Them people working in the field say she lost too much blood and whoever did it done carried her body somewhere to hide her from us. There is a curse on ma family, a curse. Bumblebee says it's called an ancestor curse. Ma children cursed. Ma land cursed. I don't have no good luck. I'm going to see Mom Dot and get to the bottom of this curse."

T-Red takes Maymay to Mom Dot, and Mom Dot tells her that the person who killed me is going to go mad and let loose. Maymay thinks that whatever Mom Dot says is gospel, and she believes it. It is the truth. She looks at the people on TV who talk about the future, and she has listened to the Revered Ike with T-Man, but she always knew that Mom Dot is the real thing. She once told Bumblebee under her tree, "The people who poor and live common closer to God than those rich people. If you want to find the real thing, look at the people living next to that old muddy bayou in those old cypress shacks like Mom Dot."

She returns from the visit and takes her seat under the huge oak tree. Everything is quiet. Many times, when she has something long and hard to think about, she goes under the tree and talks to the tree as if it is T-Man. T-Man planted the oak tree when they first bought their property years ago. She doesn't have anyone else who can talk about the old days and the old ways, when things were simple when there were no phones or fancy cars, just visitors and horses.

Maymay tells the tree, "Tut brings the biggest mess to Belle Place, but Mom Dot tells me what gon' happen. She say that man who killed Tut done an evil thing, and that thing gon' eat him up so bad, he gon' go mad. Now they're trying to find where he done hide her body. Tut was doing good in Sunset. She comes back to our cursed property just to get killed." Maymay begins to cry. "I sure wish I can see her again. I miss Tut."

Maymay hears the phone ringing in the house. She walks over to the house to answer the phone. It is the police.

"Hello, Ms. Margurite Bastille, please," an important-sounding person says.

Maymay says, "Yes, this her."

"We've found Theresa Bastille's body. We found her and her unborn child's body. They were both found in a crawfish pond six miles from your house. We are going to need someone to identify the body," The important voice says.

T-Red rushes over to Maymay's house and they drive over to identify my body. When they get there, they see that my body is blood, guts, and limbs. My unborn baby has just its skeleton. She can tell it's me by my hair and what I am wearing.

Maymay has a wake and funeral service for me and the baby. Both of what is left of us is placed in the coffin. The coffin is closed. Maymay cooks a big pot of gumbo for the family at her house. The family takes pictures in their same black outfits that they wore for T-Man's funeral. They want me to laugh again.

"Well, somebody just showed how they hate Tut. They ran her over with a tractor and dumped her body in a crawfish pond. Everybody really hates her in this town," someone says from the front porch.

Maymay says, "*Non, non*," from her rocking chair as she smokes her pipe. "If they hate her so much, why did they show up and support her?"

"Shame! Plain old shame and nosy," T-Red says as he stands like a giant next to Maymay's rocking chair. "All the *traiteurs* die a painful death. T-Man and now Tut. She knows the secrets. Now she done died a bad death."

My Celeste, who never went against T-Red, says, "T-Red, she died because of hatred. Whoever killed her is probably some man who didn't want to pay child support for Tinie or me. I'm not going to say that she deserved what she got. She didn't deserve to die, but she lived a bad life. She even took Black over us. She knew bad people. Grandpa was a good man who always tried to help people by praying on them. God would never punish someone for being good. He prayed on people, even though it made him sick. He probably died of cancer from using mouthwash on his garden or eating all of that pork meat. Don't feel bad, Grandma. Maybe she is in a better place."

Maymay is surprised that Celeste has gone against what she and T-Red says. Maymay begins to rock and goes to sleep whispering a whole new set of rosaries. It is a calm sleep. Celeste's words make her feel better: she says I am wearing those clothes in the windows and eating World's Finest Chocolate. Maymay smiles in her sleep.

Celeste goes to her room and looks through my box of belongings. Black has brought them all to Maymay's house. He says he can't do anything with them, and he and his wife have decided to get back together again.

Bumblebee marches in the house with a box of fried chicken. She is chewing on a leg when she walks in and plops on the sofa.

She tells Tiny, "Put this on the table. Papoo gave me that discount chicken." She looks over at Maymay. "She sleeping? She always sleeping. She sleep hard too. Celeste, come here. Let me tell you something."

Celeste walks in the room and sits next to Bumblebee.

"Look, Celeste, Maymay has a policy on Tut. She keeps a policy on everybody all the time. She still got one on Red. I also took out a policy on your mama just before she left to go with Black. I'm telling you this 'cause I don't want you to think I had anything to do with her death. We gonna buy us a doublewide trailer. Maymay has a $10,000 policy. We have a $20,000 policy. You and your sisters can have our old trailer. Flossy got $5,000 of your mama money. That's for you and your sisters and brothers school. I'm going to give you and the girls $500 to buy you some clothes.

"We put insurance on your mama because we knew she lived a high risk life. We always thought that Black would kill her after he found her in bed with somebody, but he didn't have to. Someone else did it. I loved Tut. I love y'all. We don't say it all the time like the white folks, but we love y'all. Don't think that it is about the money, because Red and Liver is going to end up in jail for killing Walter Lee. I damn near raised all of y'all, and you know it, Celeste. Tut lived her life the way she wanted. We gave her freedom. Everybody owe God one death. It is just her time to go. She redeemed herself, Celeste. She had a good name yonder in Sunset. People know her as the candy, popcorn, and Kool-Aid lady—not the ho of Belle Place," Bumblebee says and walks out of the door.

Three months has passed and the memory of my murder is here and there from a Diana Ross song playing on the new black radio station or to a paper from a Big Chief tablet that is left on the refrigerator or to a candy that I like so much from Smitty's store. The feelings are not as intense as they were when they first found out about my murder. They are still light flutters in the heart and small tear drops shed by Maymay in the old rocking chair that grinds that strong cypress floor.

Then one day, they smell the fresh smell of gas in the summer air and the popping of gravel. The children yell, "Company!" It is Sheriff Picard. He knocks on the porch. Maymay comes out in a dirty housedress. She is cutting okra and making roux.

"Hello, Ms. Margurite. Mind if I have a word with you?"

Maymay says, "Sure, let's go under the tree."

"I'm here to tell you about Tut. We think we found the killer."

Maymay looks up at the sky.

"It's Walter Lee, just like everyone expected. You can't hide a murder in a small town like this. He is the meanest thing in Belle Place. You know we don't have a whole lot of mean people here. Only problem is he has been on the run for a long time." Sheriff Picard says. "We went to his common law's wife's house, and she said that he done skipped town. Says he left without telling nobody. We think one of our colored deputies tipped him off. We were about to question him." Sheriff Picard wipes the sweat from his pale skin. "I'll keep in touch with you about it." He walks away and heads for his white and blue car and drives away.

Maymay says, "I'm going to make a big pot of cush cush to celebrate," Maymay walks over to the kitchen. "T-Red thank you so much for looking out for your sister."

"You know, a long time ago Tut, my dead brothers, and me all went there yonder in the fields and made a promise together. We said we would always stick together no matter what. She discouraged me through the years, but now I know that it's like you always say. She is my blood, and family stick together. No matter what! No matter what!" T-Red says this as he shakes his head back and forth and holds my Big Chief tablet in his hand. Everyone can tell that he is tearing up. "NO MATTER WHAT!" he shouts.

I take my place in Maymay's wall and in the beautiful pure blue sky.

Chapter 33

The Arrest

Bumblebee

I'm sure those child support payments were getting to be too much for Walter Lee and he just snapped. How in the world could someone drive a tractor over another human being like they a piece of sugar cane? I know that Walter Lee is evil. He nearly beat his wife to death, but I wouldn't think that he could kill another human being. We all know it's him 'cause he done skipped town. He is already paying child support for his four children with his ex-wife and one child with his ex-girlfriend.

If I find Walter Lee, I want to beat him myself. I fought mens before, and I'll beat the shit out of Walter Lee for killing Tut. Tut and me didn't see eye to eye all the time, but I loved that girl. She made us laugh all the time with her crazy self. She helped raise my kids just like I helped raise hers. We worked together like a family. Now she's gone, and I miss her.

The sun is just going down, and a fella named Dead Eye shows up at me and Red trailer. They call him Dead Eye 'cause his left eye is always closed. He and Red never did get along, so we find it strange for him to come to our house.

Dead Eye hollers for Red to come out of the house. He blows his horn. I open the door, "What do you want with my old man?" I ask.

"I'm looking for T-Red, Bumblebee, not you. Where he at?" Dead Eye asks from his red Pinto. Red comes out of the trailer from the other door. "What you want, Dead Eye? You know we don't hang?" Red says.

"I need you to come by the car. I got something important I got to tell you," Dead Eye says.

Red comes by the little car. He leans down and low. Dead Eye says, "I know we don't hang together. You don't even like me. I know all of that. But, you really need to listen and not say nothing, I mean nothing, until I'm done. I know how you people feel about your property and all since T-Man died, but I need you to listen and not get out your gun just yet. I can tell by the way you walking you got your pistol. Listen good T-Red. I don't mean you no harm."

"Well, go 'head, talk. I'm missing my *Dukes of Hazard*. It's Friday. On Friday we watch the *Dukes of Hazard* and eat hamburgers and French fries. You taking me away from my family tradition. Go 'head Dead Eye. What is it you want? I don't want to hear nothing about Tut and who you think done it. You probably gonna say it ain't yo' boy. I know y'all used to hang out back in the day before that nigger went to the pen."

"I know where Walter Lee is," Dead Eye just shouts out.

"You jiving me," Red says. "Take me to him, now."

He yells me, "Bumblebee, get a T-shirt."

He reaches over Dead Eye to open the passenger side door with his long arm. He takes out his .45 that he is hiding in his work boot. He goes on the other side of the car and gets in.

His long legs are bent over to his stomach even after he lets the seat back. He blows the horn. "Bumblebee bring me a shirt!" Red screams. I just stand in the door and listen.

Red turns and looks at Dead Eye. "Let me tell you one motherfucking thing. All these years I never studied about Tut. I know she was the bitch of Belle Place, but Tut is my kin, ho and all. I'm going to fuck that nigger up. I'm going to show him what happens when somebody run over my sister like she a thing and not a human. I'm going to beat him within an inch of his life. Then I'm going to call Picard and tell him to put that nigger under the jail house in his body bag that I'm gon' piss on."

Red says as he points the gun at Dead Eye's head, "You better not be lying to me, nigger."

One of my children hands me two shirts. I shout from the door, and tell Liver to get some guns. He begins to take guns from the gun cabinet and packs them in a duffel bag.

I grab a red Marlboro wife beater, and I go with them. If anybody is going to kick Walter Lee's ass, it's going to be me. Liver and me sit behind Dead Eye. I kick the seat in so that we have more room. Dead Eye looks like he is in a lot of pain.

Liver tosses the red T-shirt shirt to his father. "Good color. When I get that nigger's blood on it, it won't show."

"Oh yeah, you people in Belle Place think it's a game. All these years y'all messed with my family. I done time in the pen myself for fighting. If I kill this nigger, I know Picard and them will let me off, but I'm going to mutilate his privates and chew his face like chewing gum. He gon' remember what it is to mess with a Bastille I guarantee you."

"Give me your gun. I don't trust you." Red takes the gun that is on Dead Eye's lap. "Drive," T-Red shouts.

It has been raining that day. The road is wet and muddy. Dead Eye tries to speed away but is slowed down when the tires get stuck in mud.

"I knew you would come in handy, Liver," Red says. "Go out there and unbug him." Liver lifts the car out of the mud while Dead Eye gives it gas. Dead Eye's little Pinto wobbles from side to side. Liver hops back into the car.

We drive over to Dead Eye's place. When we turn the corner, we see about ten cop cars. A crowd of nosy people have gathered on the street looking and pointing. Red says, "Damn. Somebody tipped them off."

Dead Eye stops by someone everybody calls Aunt Susie's house. "Hey, what done happened?" Dead Eye asks.

Aunt Susie says, "Your old lady called the cops and told them to go to your house and that you were receiving threats. The cops came and found out that Walter Lee was back there. Walter Lee drove off and tried to get away. He was going about 100 miles an hour. He got to the bridge and went clean off the blacktop into the Bayou. He dead. He dead."

I'm upset that I couldn't kill him myself, but I'm happy. "Oh, Aunt Susie you can believe he got what he deserved. If I woulda got to him, I woulda damn near killed him. He lucky they got to him first," I say.

Aunt Susie tells me, "That's a shame for Walter Lee what he done to Tut. She shoulda stayed in Sunset. I done heard she was doing good over there. This is the most action that this community has seen in years. The lights look like a carnival on the bayou."

I look at the bayou. It looks bright and full of light on such an evil night. People stand around excited about all of the action. This is our first murder in Belle Place or Pretty Place. It doesn't seem pretty and peaceful like it used to be.

Chapter 34

Pure Sky

Celeste

When I look back at my life, I know that everyone has a dream and their way of doing things that many people don't feel is important. We all have to make difficult decisions and choices in life, and one day I made a difficult choice of becoming a *traiteur,* even though T-Red told me how he for himself witnessed the pain of the *traiteur.*

"Maymay, I want to be a *traiteur.*"

"*Mais,* what in the world are you saying?" Maymay says as she stirs her pot of gumbo.

"Maymay, I'm born again, and the *Bible* talks about the gift of laying hands. I think that I have the gift. Tut told me that you have to try it on somebody, and if they get healed, you have the gift. I've helped heal children with my mama in Sunset. I want to be a *traiteur.* I look at all of the family pictures of you and T-Man's room, and I see that no one is going to take the tradition on. T-Man gave it to Tut. Tut used her gift on the children in the trailer park, and I'm Tut's daughter, so I should carry it on, especially since Mama is no longer with us."

"You know being a *traiteur* is not like they say in the *Bible.* You have to learn how to do that from someone, and it is some language that you don't know," Maymay says.

She stops stirring her pot and sits next to me. "Bumblebee says it is not of God. She says that language and stuff come from Africa." Maymay says.

"Well, I thought about it, and everyone I know who is good is a *traiteur*. They are unselfish people who have pure hearts. Mrs. Canoe would always help us, no matter what. T-Man would treat people for no money. He would go out in the fields and woods and gather teas for people for free. Tut at times had the mind of a child, but she always tried to help people who were being charged too much. Bumblebee stole our dirt and let some strange white man pray on it. If that is not African hoodoo, I don't know what is," I say, and Maymay smiles.

"Maymay, I don't believe in curses. I only believe in God and my *Bible*. The God I know would never curse my papa or Mrs. Canoe or my mama. If he would, then I'm not serving the same God. Only I know that I know God, and he gave both of them a good life. Besides no matter what anybody says, they healed people and they have a pure heart. They will see God. Take me to Mom Dot. I want to receive the instruction."

Maymay sits at her kitchen table. It is filled with plates to be washed that Bumblebee and her children have left. Maymay says, "They never clean up after theyselves. I'll take you to Mom Dot. She is a *traiteur*. Me and Bumblebee trust her."

The next day, T-Red comes by and gives me the $3,000. It is the nicest thing that he has ever done. He takes me to Mom Dot, who goes into the room and shows me how to be a *traiteur*. Mom Dot has healed people for many years, and now I will be part of that legacy.

The Bastille family has reclaimed their good name. They have reclaimed it by claiming it themselves. Maymay says that no one can take what they never gave away. How can other people judge them?

My family is strong. They know how to work together and be strong. There is no curse on this family—no curse of the *traiteur* and no curse of the Mulatto.

Maymay tells her children and grandchildren at the family reunion, "The curse of the Mulatto and the curse of the *traiteur* is just some tale that someone who had nothing better to do with they time told. The Blessed Virgin Mary personally watches over ma house and ma family. I see that through the beautiful colors she leaves above ma house. Stories and words cannot hold this family down. Only we hold ourselves down with hate of not forgiving others."

"Celeste tells me that she asked a nun why the Blessed Mother wears that color. The nun said it is for the pure sky. The sky and the rain cleans our earth and land. Just like the tears cleans our soul," Maymay says. She prays with us under the oak tree, and everyone enjoys the feast at the family reunion.

Chapter 35

Lapis Lazuli

Maymay

When the cane was high, Celeste receives an unexpected visitor. Vashan shows up on ma porch with his mother and father. He knows that coming by ma property could cost him his life, but he do it anyway.

"Hello, Maymay. I need to speak with you. I am here for a very important matter. I want to promise my love to Celeste," he tells me. I am sitting on ma bed, smoking my pipe.

"Where is the ring?" T-Red asks.

"I have it here in my hand," Vashan says.

"Y'all come on in," T-Red says.

"No, that won't be necessary. You see, you told Vashan that you would kill him if he enters your house again. We're fine right here," Dr. Susan says.

"Let me see the ring," T-Red says as he opens the screen door. I sit on the bed next to the tulip lamp. I am going blind in one eye because I refuse to go to the doctor and fix my glaucoma. I don't trust doctors.

T-Red says, "This ring is blue. This ain't no real ring, man. What kind of racket y'all trying to run here? Maymay look at this t'ing."

I look at the ring with ma one good eye and say, "*Mais,* T-Red its blue, but it got two big diamonds on the side. They look real to me. These two diamonds here bigger than the one on ma and ma grandmother's ring put together. Why you make the main stone blue, though? What sense does that make? What that blue made out of?"

I think it's real. I read those children letters. They love each other.

"If'n this ring is as real as it looks, she is going to talk to you. I will see to it myself. That girl is going to marry this boy with his different hair and everything," I say.

I read almost all of those letters with ma good eye in this room. She threw every one of them away. She said Vashan was like Black. But, if he is coming here with his people, he is like the man who shared this bed with me. Those letters had a lot of passion, and if you want to promise her, I think she should take you serious 'cause you not playing around. A long tear rolls out of ma blind eye as I think about T-Man.

Vashan will be dancing with Celeste under the oak tree underneath that pure blue sky that they used to always write about before Celeste stopped writing back to him. They are going to dance just like me *et* T-Man did. I smile when I think about their love and me and T-Man love.

I knock at T-Red's old trailer. "Celeste, I need to speak with you," I say. "There is someone here to see you. I am not going to cut corners. It's Vashan, and he wants to see you. He want to give you a promise ring. I am your Maymay, and I think that you should see him. I want you to see him. You can do what you want, but that is what I want you to do. All of them letters you threw away meant nothing, but a man standing on ma porch after T-Red and me both said that we both was going to kill him and meant it deserves your high time. He bringing his family here to meet us. He must really like you. Talk to him. Any man willing to risk his life for you will protect and work for you and your children. They gon' give you your own house with your blue sky and your tulip lamp with your books and everything else. That's all I'm gon' say. That's what I would do. Do you want that passion he put on your face? Stop being afraid of it. Go meet that fella."

Vashan screams, "And reaching up my hand to try, I screamed to feel it touch the sky." He holds the ring up to the sky. There in the sky, in his hands, is the blue ring with diamonds on the side.

"Celeste, I am eighteen years old now, and I can make my own decisions. I want you to join me at Harvard. My father went through a lot of trouble to get this stone. It comes from Afghanistan. It is a lapis lazuli. It represents the Blessed Mother and her pure blue sky," Vashan says as he reaches for Celeste's hand and gets down on one knee.

"Will you promise to try to love me me?"

"I will," Celeste says.

He lifts Celeste and runs through the fields. "Y'all be careful. Come back. Y'all not married yet!" I shout.

Chapter 36

Celeste's and Vashan's Sky

Celeste

That summer, Maymay builds a covered gazebo big enough to entertain our family and friends. We have a big *fais do-do* for both families to celebrate our promise. I call our promise a promise to the sky. The sky holds our God, our ancestors, and everything we behold greater than ourselves. Our promise is to them to continue our bloodline and our love. It's a promise to continue our bloodline and our love. It's not about the ring or the fact that his family is at my house. I know that he loves me by the way he looks at me. I think that I never thought that I was good enough for someone like Vashan, but I know that nothing can take me away from his love and our passion.

"Celeste, I know that you are probably wondering why I did not attend the funeral," Amy says. "I don't say goodbye that way. I never go to funerals. I remember Tut as a revolutionary, just like all of those people you read about. Her ideas were new. Who could start a business from a shopping cart? Everybody is trying to sell things like your mom and Flossy did. The only thing is that Tut was so much fun to be around. People would buy from her just because they liked her." She hugs me.

Flossy says, "Celeste, your Maymay has turned this place into something special. Who has a huge gazebo and a dance floor in the middle of nowhere? This place looks really special. I am proud of you, Celeste. I feel bad that Tut can't enjoy this day, but I can't say I spend a lot of time crying because I know that she died after she saw her dreams come true. Black is going to tow Tut's broken Volkswagen and put it in front of the dance floor." We hug each other. Both Amy and Flossy are happy for me. Flossy is now driving an ice cream truck with a sign that reads "Flossy's Soul Food."

Dr. Matthews flies his family members in from Jamaica. These are the ones that Vashan says knew Bob Marley.

"What do you want to dance to first?" Maymay asks.

"I want to dance to 'Redemption Song' in honor of my mother," I say.

As they play the music, Vashan's uncles remove their multi-colored hats that cover their long dreads. Their dreads swing wild and free in some uncanny dance in pure blue sky in unison. Their locks are long and free like our passion. I hold Vashan. I feel like everything is coming together, and we are one with this magnificent universe. He kisses me and we dance underneath the pure blue sky.

Acknowledgement

I would like to acknowledge several people, including my wonderful husband Melvin Collins and my children who were denied several good home-cooked meals due to my writing and dreaming about being a published writer. Thanks to my mom and dad who made sure that I was educated with the little money they had. They always encouraged me to read and write. All of my wonderful brothers and sisters have always supported my writing, as well. I would like to thank my aunts and uncles, including my Uncle Paul, Aunt Gloria, Aunt Mary Lynn, and Aunt Theresa, for inspiring me with their wisdom and love. I dedicate this book to my Uncle Romiere, who took time to tell me stories and folktales. There is an African proverb that says when an ancestor dies, it's like burying a library. Uncle Romiere is no longer with us, but his stories still remain with me.

I would like to thank my fellow writers from Alvar's Writer's Group, including Lee Grue and Helen Krieger for their instruction and encouragement when I attended their workshops. I would like to acknowledge my writing family in New York, including Brenda Green, Clarence Reynolds, and J.I. Torres. I thank and celebrate my fellow sister writers from The Center of Black Literature Fellows: Keisha Gaye, Elaine Frasier, Emma Jappo, and Kerika Fields. Thanks to Ernesto Quionez, who taught a fiction seminar.

A special thanks to Michael Sartisky who published an excerpt from my novel, "The Curse of the Mulatto" in the 2009 issue of the magazine Louisiana Cultural Vistas. The article was absolutely beautiful with the breath-taking photographs taken by Cheryl Gerber. A special thanks to writers I met on the Louisiana Book

Festival Panel entitled Upcoming Novels, the very talented Moira Crone and Jamey Hatley. I have kept contact with them through the years.

Thanks to the University of Louisiana who invited me to speak during English week about my upcoming novel. Thanks to all of those who help promote the Louisiana Creole culture in Louisiana, including Mo Creole, Christophe Landry, Elroy Batiste, Charles Jolivette, and the Louisiana Endowment for the Humanities.

Thanks to those who helped me with my blog. I couldn't have done it without my cousin Angie Serrano. Thanks for the music provided by William Elder and Keith Frank.

Thanks to Gail Diamond who wrote my first review. Thanks to Rosemary James and the William Faulkner Society. The William Faulkner William Wisdom competition is a wonderful writing contest that fills writers with so much hope.

All of you mentioned and many who are not mentioned have filled my Celestial Blue Sky with hope, love, laughter, and most of all, inspiration. Thanks to everyone who shared my enthusiasm about this novel. I hope that it enlightens your life as much as it has enlightened mine.

About the Author

Maggie Collins was born and raised under the clear blue skies of Loreauville, Louisiana. She majored in English at the University of Louisiana and later earned a Master's degree from the University of New Orleans. An excerpt of this novel was published in "Louisiana Cultural Vistas" and was a 2009 finalist for the worldwide William Faulkner William Wisdom writing contest. She is a Center for Black Literature fellow and an Educational Diagnostician. She lives with her two sons and wonderful husband.